Montbel

A Jacques Forêt Mystery

Angela Wren

www.darkstroke.com

Discover us online:
www.darkstroke.com

Join us on facebook:
www.facebook.com/groups/darkstroke

Tweet a photo of yourself holding
this book to **@darkstrokedark**
and something nice will happen.

For the elderly gentleman I met in La Ferté-Macé (61), a time-control location on the *Tour de Normandie*, who shared with me a brief glimpse of his childhood in occupied France.

Acknowledgments

My very grateful thanks go to:

Dave Bastow, retired Green Watch Crew Manager of West Yorkshire Fire and Rescue Service, for his invaluable advice, guidance and his patience in answering all my questions.

My writing colleagues, who have patiently listened, have answered my searching questions, and encouraged me when my faith in my story faltered.

Carol, a reader, who suggested the inclusion of a glossary.

My editor and publisher, without whom this would not have been possible.

About the Author

Angela Wren is an actor and director at a small theatre a few miles from where she lives in the county of Yorkshire in the UK. She worked as a project and business change manager – very pressured and very demanding – but she managed to escape, and now she writes books.

She has always loved stories and story-telling, so it seemed a natural progression, to her, to try her hand at writing, starting with short stories. Her first published story was in an anthology, which was put together by the magazine 'Ireland's Own' in 2011.

Angela particularly enjoys the challenge of plotting and planning different genres of work. Her short stories vary between contemporary romance, memoir, mystery, and historical. She also writes comic flash-fiction and has drafted two one-act plays that have been recorded for local radio.

Her full-length stories are set in France, where she likes to spend as much time as possible each year.

Follow Angela at **www.angelawren.co.uk** and **www.jamesetmoi.blogspot.co.uk**.

The Jaques Forêt Mystery series by Angela Wren:

Messandrierre (#1)
Merle (#2)
Montbel (#3)
Marseille (#4)

Montbel

A Jacques Forêt Mystery

la lettre

...families fracture, Monsieur Forêt. No one desires it or intends it, but it happens. A harsh, unforgiving word begets a rash and revengeful action, and a sliver of ice takes hold in a dark corner of the hearts of those at odds with each other. And there it wedges itself, the frost gradually deepening and destroying. One of us has to stop the cold, as this impasse can continue no longer.
I have to put things right with my son, Monsieur...

june 3rd, 2011

wednesday, june 8th

In his office in Mende, Jacques Forêt, now Principal Investigator and Managing Director of Vaux Investigations, scanned through the documents in the various files in front of him. He flipped the card cover of the last one closed. Open and shut case, he thought as he tapped his forefinger on the desk and wondered why he'd bothered to accept the commission in the first place. Pushing his chair back, he strolled over to the floor to ceiling windows and looked down on the street below. In the bright morning sunshine, people scurried backwards and forwards as they went about their business. Across the street sat the sister building that housed the second company, Vaux Consulting, within the family-owned group. He grinned as he reflected on how lucky he had been to assume his current role so quickly after commencing work with the organisation. It was the successful investigation into the deaths in the suburb of Merle – and the internal fraud connected with that particularly complex case – that had been the springboard for his early and meteoric promotion.

A tap at his office door brought him back to the present.

"Bruno, good to see you again and thanks for coming over." Jacques shook his visitor's hand, a broad and welcoming smile on his face.

"I don't remember you having this office when we last worked together, Jacques," said Investigating Magistrate Bruno Pelletier as he took the chair indicated and grinned.

"No. There have been a number of changes all across the Vaux Group, but I'm still here, and so is Alain Vaux. He heads up the business consulting arm of Vaux now and is Chairman of the Board at group level. It's all very corporate, Bruno, and I'm still not used to that. I don't think

4

I ever will be. But, there are some old habits that I will never change," he said, nodding to the vast whiteboard that he'd had fitted to the wall directly opposite his desk. "A whiteboard was good enough for us when I was on investigations in Paris, and it still works for me here."

Bruno sighed. "Once a policeman, always a policeman, eh, Jacques?" He turned back to the board. "A lot of names up there. Business must be good."

"Yes. We're doing very well. A lot of missing person cases, some connected with inheritances. A few matrimonial issues for which we're gathering evidence of infidelity, or not, as is necessary. A couple of hunting fatalities that are going nowhere at the moment; and three re-examinations of old police investigations. It's one of those that I want to discuss with you."

Bruno removed his rimless spectacles and began to polish them with his handkerchief. "As I said on the phone, I'm happy to help if I can."

Jacques ran his hand through his thick dark brown hair. "Thanks. The fire at the restaurant in Montbel, two years ago. I need a bit of background…"

"There's not a lot to tell you," Bruno said as he donned his glasses and shrugged.

Jacques pulled his notebook towards him, ready to make notes and waited.

"As I recall it, arson was suspected from the outset and proven for the destruction of the building," said Bruno.

Jacques nodded and scribbled a note. "And where was the seat of the fire?"

"In the store room coming off the kitchen. According to the Fire Investigation Officer's report, there were large plastic bottles full of oil in there that would have fuelled the fire and that would have enabled the blaze to take hold quickly and then burn for a significant period, sufficient for it to ignite the fabric of the building and once that had happened the place was beyond saving."

"Can you remember who contacted the fire service?"

Bruno folded his arms and thought for a moment. "The

owner, Étienne Vauclain. At the time, he lived about 700 hundred metres away on Grande Rue at the edge of the village."

"What about the person who died there?"

"Ah…yes. That was an unfortunate tragedy. The Fire Chief in charge of the blaze was firmly assured by Vauclain that the building was empty. The Fire Chief openly admitted that, had he known there was someone in there, he would have handled things differently." Bruno paused and shook his head.

"And the body, when it was discovered…"

"Male, he was found face down, but with the usual pugilistic pose, on the floor between the kitchen and the dining room. The appearance was that he had been trying to reach safety. According to the autopsy report, his lungs were filled with smoke and he probably died of suffocation. His body was very badly burned as a result of the advancing flames, which consumed his clothes, and most of the flesh and sinew from his back and each side of his body. His head was turned to his left and the exposed half of his face was completely destroyed. There was very little to go on for a formal identification other than the information from witnesses and the damaged remains of the wallet that was found under the body."

Jacques stopped making notes and stared at the floor, lost in thought. Fixing his gaze on the Magistrate, he frowned.

"Under the body? Are you sure about that? Doesn't that strike you as odd?"

Bruno grimaced. "Perhaps, but what are you thinking, Jacques?"

"That the wallet would most likely have been in his back pocket, and therefore, I would have expected it to be very badly damaged, or possibly destroyed, along with his clothes."

"No, it was definitely under the body. The victim was an itinerant worker and the speculation at the time was that he was most probably sleeping. The smoke and his inability to breathe would have woken him and he would have, as an automatic reflex, picked up his wallet and run or crawled to the door in an effort to get out. He didn't make it and collapsed, his right hand was clutching the wallet under his body which provided a measure of protection."

Jacques tapped his pen against his notebook. "Why was he there in the first place?"

"According to Vauclain, he was there because it was July, the busiest period for the restaurant. Extra staff were regularly employed, on a casual basis, in the kitchen during the main holiday period. The man who died was known to the chef and had worked for him before. According to witness statements, he camped locally or stayed with other kitchen staff. It wasn't unusual for him to sleep on the floor at the back without telling anyone and to be discovered the following morning by the cleaner or the chef who both came in early. He had his own rucksack and sleeping bag."

"And the identification of the body... I presume that wasn't in doubt at the time?"

"Of course not, Jacques! The witness reports were water-tight."

Jacques noticed the hardening of his visitor's tone. "I'm sorry to press you, Bruno, but I have accepted this commission, and I must make sure that I cover all possibilities." He got up and moved across to the coffee-machine. "What would you like?"

Bruno let out a sigh. "I'd like a cappuccino but my wife has insisted that I lose some weight," he said, rubbing his hand across his ample girth. "Instead, I'll have an americano." As an afterthought he added, "And sugar is not allowed, either."

Turning away to hide the smirk on his face, Jacques busied himself with the drinks and returned to his desk.

Bruno picked up the teaspoon, hesitated and replaced it in the saucer. "So, are you going to tell me more about your interest in this case?"

"I'm just making enquiries for a client, Bruno." He flipped his notebook shut. "But, if you are certain of the identity of the body that was found, then I don't think there is much more that I can do." He sat back in his chair and sipped his coffee. "I don't suppose there was any hint of—"

"Murder or man-slaughter?" Bruno cut him off. "Is that your angle?"

Jacques shook his head. "Not really. It's just that I can't help wondering if there was something going on behind the scenes. I know that Luc Nowak was convicted for the torching of the restaurant. I also know that he can be, and has been, hired for setting fire to other business properties in the area. If you remember, he was also found guilty and sent down for the damage done at another location in Mende a few months later that year." Jacques took a gulp of coffee and returned his cup to the saucer with a clatter.

"Yes, I see where you are going with this. Collusion between Nowak and the owner was not proven, Jacques. We could find no evidence to link the two."

Jacques noticed that his visitor was cleaning his spectacles again. "No evidence," he repeated. "But, perhaps you sensed there was something at the time, maybe?"

Bruno let out a short, muffled laugh. "Ah... You know me too well! But you're right. I did suspect there might have been some collusion, but I could not substantiate it. At the time of the investigation, I thought that Vauclain knew more than he was telling us. But there was no evidence." The magistrate threw his hands up in the air. "What can I do when there's no evidence? Nothing! I was wrong."

Jacques saw how weary and defeated his previous colleague looked. The colour of his eyes had paled, and a dark frown furrowed his forehead. "We all get it wrong sometimes, Bruno."

"I know. Maybe it's time for me to admit I'm not up to the job any longer. My wife would be very happy if I did." He drained the dregs of his coffee and stood. "I have to go," he said glancing at his watch. "If you need anything else, just call me."

The lunchtime business in the restaurant in the nearby village of Messandrierre had been brisk but the number of customers had dwindled to half a dozen or so as Jacques finished the final morsel of cheese and drained the last of the Merlot from his glass.

"Coffee, Jacques?" Gaston collected the empty plate as he swept by the table.

"And can we have that chat, too?"

Gaston nodded his response, went straight to the bar and made two coffees. A few moments later he was seated opposite Jacques.

"The restaurant in Montbel, Gaston. What can you tell me about it?"

Gaston stroked his thumb and forefinger over his drooping moustache before answering.

"Not that much," he said. "Marianne dealt with Vauclain, that was the owner, and she spent a lot of time talking to the chef when he first came. She wanted to make sure that the impact on our business of that place opening was kept to the minimum."

"And did their opening affect your income?"

"At first, a little. But that was novelty value, I suppose. People trying the place just because it was somewhere new."

"When was that?"

Gaston thought for a moment. "The new *Salle des Fêtes* here in the village was finished in 2002, and I think the restaurant in Montbel opened the following April."

Jacques made a note. "So, the place was only open for six years, then?"

"Not exactly, no."

Jacques waited as Gaston savoured his coffee and then cradled the cup in his hands.

"That first summer, in 2003, they were open six days a week – like us – and they did very well, according to village gossip. Vauclain decided he would extend his opening period into the autumn. He wanted to take advantage of all the hunting parties that we get, and to try and build up a regular clientele."

Jacques looked up from his notebook. "That's your

source of business in the autumn, Gaston. How did that go down with you and Marianne?"

Gaston shrugged. "Business is business, Jacques. The hunting parties book through us because they use the chalets or the campsite here in Messandrierre. In Montbel, there are only five *gîtes* scattered across the village for them to use. Here, we have everything in one location. In Montbel, they don't. As a business plan, his idea was not very carefully thought out. We continued to get our usual level of bookings, so we took most of the hunting parties' business, and he closed the restaurant..." Gaston thought for a moment. "...in November, I think. Towards the end of November." He nodded as if to assure himself that he was correct.

"Then what?"

"The following year he restricted his business opening from April to the end of October, and he spent a lot of money getting some plans for an extension prepared. He thought that, if he could get a large function room, similar to our *Salle des Fêtes*, he could encourage business people to use the space during the week, and at weekends it could be used for celebrations and weddings. That sort of thing. But..."

"Turned down?" suggested Jacques.

The last two diners shouted their goodbyes, and Gaston got up and went over to them. Jacques took a mouthful of his lukewarm coffee and grimaced. He shoved the almost full cup and saucer away and began flicking back through his notes.

"Jacques, bring the cups and we'll talk at the bar." Gaston locked the door behind his final customers. Back at the bar, he set about making some fresh coffee.

"Vauclain's plan... Thinking about the place in Montbel on the couple of occasions when I went there, I'm guessing his idea never came to fruition."

Gaston put a small black coffee on the bar for Jacques and poured himself one. "Depends on which one you mean, Jacques. He kept changing his plans. The function room was replaced with a plan to turn the place into a small boutique hotel. But that upset a lot of local people. We objected. The owners of the small hotels in Badaroux and Châteauneuf-de-Randon also objected." Gaston sat on the stool behind the bar and ran his nicotine-stained fingers through his long greying hair. "In 2007, I think it was, he just seemed to withdraw. Or, he may have decided to just let the place run itself for a while. Anyway, he took less and less interest. His chef left without notice, and he closed right at the end of August that year. The next year was very good for us all. But Vauclain still wasn't taking much interest. His new chef left at the end of the season and refused to come back the following year."

"So he missed an opportunity to sell the place then as a going concern."

"That's right, which is why I think the fire was a put-up job. And I wasn't the only one, if the gossip at the time was anything to go by."

Jacques put his notebook down and a frown gathered on his forehead. "The conclusion in the Fire Officer's report is that it was arson, and we already have a conviction, Gaston. What exactly are you getting at?"

Gaston took out his cigarettes and reached for the small ashtray that he kept hidden under the bar. "Do you mind?"

Jacques shook his head.

The cigarette lit, he took a long drag and exhaled. "I heard that Vauclain had a number of disagreements with his last chef. The chef wanted to revamp the menu, but that was refused. The chef then suggested that they offer specials on particularly busy days during the week. That idea was also refused." Gaston flicked the ash from the cigarette into the ashtray. "Marianne was over there one day and heard them arguing about the future of the business, and Vauclain said something along the lines of, 'It's my business, I'll do as I damn well please.' Apparently, the chef then accused him of running his business into the ground for his own purposes. I can't remember the precise words Marianne used back then, but that was what she meant."

"How does that support your theory that the fire was set deliberately?"

"The rumour was that Vauclain had used the accounts from 2008, the very good year, to go to a new insurance company and get a much better deal with a larger pay-out in the event of anything catastrophic happening. In 2009, he closed the restaurant partway through the season again because of differences with his chef. It was a couple of days later that the place burnt down. It seems quite straightforward to me, Jacques."

His interest piqued, Jacques stared at the mirrored back wall of the bar and mentally skimmed through the pages of collected information in his office files. The insurance company had paid out, no questions asked, once the Fire Officer's report had been received and the police investigation had concluded. Jacques checked his notes. The arrest of the arsonist was made on November 3rd, 2009. The case was heard in 2010 and the perpetrator, Luc Nowak, sent down, his sentence to run consecutively to an existing period of incarceration awarded for the fire he started at the back of a property in Mende. The property that had now become Beth's photographic studio and shop.

"It's quite a leap, Gaston, from arson to collusion." Jacques shifted on his barstool. "Nowak was a loner. Always worked alone. He has a string of convictions stretching back to when he was 14 years old, and at no time has anyone else ever been implicated and convicted alongside him on the same charges." Jacques fixed Gaston with a narrow-eyed stare.

"I can only tell you what I've heard and what I think, Jacques," Gaston shrugged his comment away.

"Hmm... And how do you know that the police investigation didn't look at that, anyway? It was Magistrate Pelletier who handled the case, and he wouldn't have missed a possibility like that."

Gaston stubbed out his cigarette. "You do know that the chef wanted to buy Vauclain out, don't you?"

That wasn't in any of the reports or statements I looked

at. Jacques nodded, keeping his thoughts at bay as he pocketed his notebook and stood. "Thanks, Gaston. I'll leave it at that for now."

*** *** ***

Beth was agonising over her list of invitees. *Should I send one to Richard Delacroix or not?* She turned her neatly written sheet of paper over and back again, and sighed.

"Well, if I don't he will be the only person in the village who isn't invited," she said to herself. Looking to the *pâtisserie* across the road from the property that she was leasing in Mende, she thought back to Delacroix's first arrival in Messandrierre for his uncle's funeral. She scowled when she recalled his very direct look as he had walked past her on his way back to the chalet he had rented from Marianne. *Well, Monsieur Delacroix, that look was not at all appropriate.* A catalogue of incidents, which began with Delacroix failing to attend the buffet in the village restaurant immediately following the funeral, flooded her mind.

"You really upset the whole village that day." She shook her head and stared at his name, which was last on her list. Harsh and threatening words echoed through her conscious as she replayed the argument in the bar between *Fermier* Rouselle and Delacroix. Rouselle consistently offering less and less for the price per head for Delacroix's inherited herd of Aubracs, whilst Delacroix raised it. Then there was the disruption in the village caused by the dismantling of the barn and the building of the extension to the old farmhouse that Delacroix had also inherited. All of which had prompted a series of disgruntled conversations between Madame Pamier and Marianne over a number of months. Subsequently, each conversation had been repeated throughout the village at every opportunity.

Beth closed her eyes and tried to shake the acrimonious memories from her mind. Her decision finally made, she scrubbed his name off the list. Collecting together the cards already written, she slotted them into the previously addressed envelopes. Part way through her task she paused. *If I don't invite him, I'm making a very public statement, which will not be missed by anyone in Messandrierre.* She stared at the blank computer screen on the counter as her thoughts veered between the extremes of yes or no. In a determined frenzy, she added Delacroix to the list again, scribbled out another invitation, enveloped it, sealed and addressed it before she had time to change her decision again.

"I doubt he'll come anyway, and at least I can say, if anyone asks, that he was invited." Smiling to herself, she tidied the envelopes into three separate piles. Those for addresses in the village she slotted into her briefcase. She would deliver them at the weekend when she and Jacques were back at the chalet. The ones to be posted she put on one side and the ones to be taken to the neighbouring businesses in the street and the local printer, she propped up against her computer screen. A knock on the glass of the front door to the photographic studio and shop made Beth look up in surprise. A smile of recognition crossed her face and she went to the door, turned the key and opened it.

"And these must be my full-length prints of the landscapes for the front window, are they?" She indicated the large cardboard tube that the printer was carrying through the door.

Monsieur Rochefort laid his burden carefully on the counter. "Yes, and I'm very pleased with how your photographs have turned out. As you know, I was concerned that we might lose some of the sharpness in the detail." His smile beamed through his bushy grey beard and moustache. "I think the one for autumn is the best," he said as he began to pull out the tight roll of prints. He gently lowered the precious cargo to the floor, knelt down, and let the long and narrow vinyl banners unfurl.

"Those colours in the spring blossoms are spectacular," he said as Beth remained standing and took in the whole picture. Moving to the side of the floor-to-ceiling banner, he

14

gently pulled it towards himself to reveal the one beneath.

Beth smiled with self-satisfaction. "The blue of that sky has come out beautifully," she said. "But it's the art work for autumn that I particularly want to see."

Monsieur Rochefort obliged, and it was a few moments before either of them spoke.

"The colours in the canopies' of the trees are stunning," said Beth. As her eyes moved over the content of the picture a wide smile formed on her face. "And Pierre looks totally enthralled."

"It was a fabulous photo to work from."

"I don't know if I will be able to use it, though. Pierre's *maman* knows about it and is quite keen that I do, but I got that shot two years ago when Pierre was only six. He hasn't seen it yet, and he's eight now." She smiled at her visitor. "Eight going on eighty-eight, and he's developing some quite fixed opinions of his own. He may not like it."

The printer smiled back. "I hope he agrees. It's a stunning photograph and the way you have contrasted the black, white and grey central panel of the road, Pierre and the bike against the flanking red, yellow and gold of the trees..." He sighed. "It's inspired." Moving the banner to one side, he revealed the final picture, a snowy landscape.

"Perfect," said Beth. "Can you show me how to hang them now or do you need to be somewhere else, Monsieur Rochefort?"

"We'll do it now," he said and moved over to the full-length window to check the fittings on the ceiling and the floor. As Monsieur Rochefort took a preliminary look at the fittings, Beth retrieved the envelope addressed in his name.

"I hope you will be able to come to the formal opening of the shop next week," she said as she handed him the envelope.

15

thursday, june 9ᵗʰ

The village of Montbel was some eight kilometres from
Messandrierre. Sitting at the centre of an expanse of high
pasture, it was surrounded by a series of fenced off areas.
From some, the large ancient boulders that had been
deposited across the landscape as the ancient ice sheets had
retreated had been removed and casually left in out-of-the-
way corners of the enclosures. These open spaces were
cultivated with crops growing tall and pear-green in the
early summer sunshine. Other spaces were occupied by
small groups of Aubrac cattle whose sole purpose for their
days seemed to be to graze, to sit for hours, and to graze
again.

The D6, which stretched eastwards from the main
interchange between Mende and Le Puy-en-Velay, sliced the
village of Montbel in two as it meandered its way across the
high valley to a final junction in La Bastide-Puylaurent. The
sign on the wall of the first house on the right announced
that the numbered, but nameless, road became Grande Rue
at that point. Jacques slowed down and looked to his left
and, as described, a long stone barn stood end on to the
street. In front of it was a large enclosed area with black-
and gold-painted metal fencing set into a low stone wall.
Jacques pulled up, removed his helmet and wheeled his
motorbike across the road, down the short track in front of
the converted barn, and into the beautifully planted front
garden. He rested his bike on the steady just inside the main
gate and placed his helmet on the seat.

"Monsieur Forêt, I presume?" Étienne Vauclain rose
from his patio chair and walked towards Jacques.

"Call me Jacques," he said as he shook Vauclain's

outstretched hand.

The man was much shorter than Jacques had imagined, his hair, thick and grey, was swept back and expensive dark glasses hid his eyes. Jacques followed him to the patio area and took a seat at the table in the shade.

"Coffee?" Vauclain steadily pushed the plunger of the *cafetière* to the bottom of the large pot.

"Yes, please." Jacques glanced past his interviewee and through the open French windows into the house. The windows on the far side of the building were shuttered against the sun, but despite the interior gloom, Jacques could make out a gallery that he assumed ran the full length of the building. Above, he could see the edges of the beams of the roof and within the body of the visible space, comfortable and very fashionable furnishings.

"On the phone yesterday, you said I may be able to help you with some enquiries," said Vauclain as he pushed a cup and saucer across the table to Jacques.

"I believe you knew a Monsieur Antoine Beaufort." Jacques flipped open his notebook.

Vauclain frowned and shook his head. "Beaufort? The name seems familiar, but I can't recall why."

Jacques sipped his coffee and narrowed his eyes. "Antoine Beaufort, he worked for you as a casual kitchen employee in your restaurant?" He watched him closely.

"Beaufort..." Vauclain removed his sunglasses and placed them on the table. "I remember now. The victim of the restaurant fire. That was...unfortunate." He shifted back in his chair. "A terrible accident."

"What can you tell me about Monsieur Beaufort?"

"No more than I said during the investigation into the fire and the death. He was known to my chef at the time; he was employed on a casual basis, and I did not know he had been given permission to sleep on the premises whenever he chose."

Jacques tapped his pen against his notebook and stared at Vauclain. *That's a very pat statement, Monsieur. I wonder how long it took you to get that exactly right.* He decided on a different tack.

"I have no interest in the enquiry into the fire. That case has been closed. My current enquiry is about the man himself: where he was, who he met, where he worked. I have been retained to find out what his history was, up to the date of his death."

Vauclain shrugged. "I see. And again, I'm not sure I can help you."

Jacques took a sip of his coffee and smiled. "Perhaps we can start with some facts. Can you tell me how long Beaufort worked for you?"

"Not precisely," he said. "I kept all the employment records in the office at the restaurant, and they were destroyed. I think Beaufort first visited the restaurant asking for work in May…End of May beginning of June, when I wasn't hiring. He came back a couple of weeks later, and it was the chef who hired him. I think that was at the end of June or very beginning of July."

"Whilst he was employed by you, did he work every day?"

"I can't be sure of that without the records. I know he had no skills and was just used to wash up, clean up and for general prep, that's all."

"General prep means what?"

"Washing and peeling vegetables, fetching and carrying, menial tasks to support all of the kitchen staff."

"So, as far as you know, he was never used to wait on tables or anything else?"

"As I said, he had no skills. He'd also been living rough, and it would not have been appropriate to employ him in any other capacity."

Jacques drained his coffee cup, replaced it, pushed the saucer to one side and looked Vauclain straight in the eye. "One last question. Your chef at the time, can you tell me where he is now?"

"Mende. He lives and works in Mende at the Hôtel Claustres. He's Head Chef there."

"Thank you. I'll see myself out." Jacques rose, put his

notebook away and, with a nod to Vauclain, strode down the path back to his bike. As he put his helmet on, something reflected in one of the mirrors on the bike caught his eye. Jacques, astride the machine, rocked it from its steady and stared at the right-hand mirror. He watched as Vauclain took out his phone and placed a call. *I wonder what that conversation is all about and what you're not telling me, Monsieur Vauclain.* The bike's engine roared, and he moved down the track towards the road.

***

At his recently completed and newly-extended farmhouse in Messandrierre, Richard Laurent Delacroix was moving boxes, old suitcases, and a small locked trunk down into the refitted and decorated cellar. It was now divided into two sections. A small, closed area at the back in which he had racks for wine, and the much larger central section which was furnished like a boardroom from a modern, cosmopolitan, city office block. One wall held a number of monitors that were linked to a bank of computers. In the main body of the area was a large glass topped desk with what had been described by the office supplies company as a 'Luxury Executive' leather chair. Down the centre of the remaining space was an oval glass table capable of seating 6 people.

Delacroix hefted the trunk down the last few steps of the new steel and glass panelled staircase and placed it on the dark red granite floor tiles that had been delivered and laid the month before. He returned for the last of the boxes and then mounted the stairs a third time and came back carrying a large rectangular package which he leaned up against the wall opposite his desk. The 'feature wall', as the interior designer had termed it, was covered with a textured paper and painted the same hue of red as the floor. He carefully leaned the package against the vinyl. He would hang the painting later but first he needed to measure up the job.

He was about to collect his tool box from his personal

cave when the central monitor lit up with a pale blue screen saver and the monotone electronic sound of one of the computers told him an internet call was being channelled to him.

He moved to his desk and tapped the keyboard to receive the call. The monitor on his desk changed to a plain black screen, which framed a close up of a tanned smiling face with gleaming blue eyes and a full head of black hair going grey at the temples.

"Wes, hi there!" Delacroix, Ricky to his close friends, adjusted the volume on the internal speakers, pulled out the chair and made himself comfortable.

"Hey, Ricky. That place of yours is looking real good from here." His soft Carolina twang made Delacroix smile.

"Thanks, have a real-good look," he said as he swivelled the monitor round and then back to face himself.

"Nice. Swanky. I bet that cost a packet."

"Yeah. Just a bit." He glanced around his new domain. "It's taken a good while longer than planned to get this place straight, but, yeah, it's pretty much as I envisaged it. So, to business, Wes. What have you got for me?"

"Five new clients, seven completions netting 18,500 Canadian dollars. Balance after my cut is already in your business account."

"OK, I'm liking the sound of that. Anything else?"

"Yeah. I've identified another six possible clients, and I've made an initial approach to the first of those, but the response so far is very cool."

Delacroix raised his eyebrows and grinned. "A cool response?" He shook his head in mock dismay. "You're losing your touch, old man!"

"Hey, less of the old! And trust me, I'll wheel this lady in."

Delacroix nodded. "I'm sure you will. And how is life treating you over there in Dubai?"

"It's sweet, Ricky, real sweet." A wide grin crossed his face.

Delacroix smiled and nodded. The unspoken, but shared,

knowledge needing no further explanation.

"I've got some commodities that will be coming up for onward sale in a week or so, and I think the Arab market is the perfect place for these goods," said Delacroix.

"OK. How much are we talking?"

"Total value is 210,000 US dollars, but I'm looking to get a mark-up of between 25% and 35%, and I think that particular market can stand that. So, I'm expecting you to take a third of the stock and to look for buyers in the upper income brackets. People with connections to the various branches of the royal family there would be very attractive as potential buyers."

"OK. That's no problem and if you can send me the details I'll get onto it straight away."

Delacroix tapped away at the second keyboard on his desk. "Details on the way."

"OK. Thanks, and we'll talk next month, OK?"

"Yeah. Same time next month."

Delacroix tapped his keyboard and the screen changed again, and as he moved back across the room to the *cave* the screen saver gradually grew out from the centre of the monitor.

***

At a little after four in the afternoon, Jacques was waiting in the foyer of the Hôtel Claustres for the chef, Jonnie Berger, to join him. He was just about to ask reception to remind the chef that he was still waiting when he saw a tall man, wearing a pristine chef's jacket and black trousers, walking towards him. Jacques stood and they shook hands.

"What can I do for you, Monsieur Forêt?"

"I'm making enquiries into the history of Antoine Beaufort before his death in the restaurant fire in Montbel in 2009. I understand that you worked there at the time, and that Monsieur Beaufort was employed by you to work in the kitchens."

Jonnie sat back and smiled. "That's right. I'd known

Antoine for about, what nine or ten years by then."

Jacques raised an eyebrow. "That's interesting. How did you first meet Monsieur Beaufort?"

The chef paused for a moment. "It was in Orléans. I was *Chef de Partie* on *pâtisserie* at a medium-sized hotel there, and Antoine came to work in the kitchens over the summer." Another pause.

"Yes?"

"Orléans. That's where we first met."

Jacques pressed on. "And can you be precise about when. Was it 1999 or 2000?"

"July 2000."

"And he was working with you for how long then?"

"All summer."

Jacques dumped his notebook and pen on the table and sat back. "Monsieur Berger, I'm not a policeman anymore. I'm a private investigator. I've been retained by my client to find out as much as I can about Monsieur Beaufort. I'm not here to question what happened in the fire. That case is closed. I just want to collect details of Monsieur Beaufort's life for my client. I know that the relationship between Monsieur Beaufort and his family was strained, and that he left home when he was 18 following an argument. I just want to piece together the details of his life since then. That's all."

Jonnie nodded and a half-smile crossed his face. "OK," he said. "I only know what he told me about his family and why he left, and he didn't say that much."

"But he said something?"

"Only that his older brother was the family favourite and that everything was organised around him, his inheritance of the family business and the *château*. He just got tired of it and he left."

"Did he tell you anything of what he had done, or how he had lived between leaving home and turning up in Orléans?"

Jonnie thought for a moment. "Nothing specific that I can remember. I got the impression that he had just drifted from place to place and menial job to job."

Jacques nodded. "And what about when he was working with you?"

"He was just employed as a *plongeur* and *marmiton* rather than to actually work with me. But he was clearly interested in *pâtisserie*, and he had knowledge of the subject too. A surprising knowledge for someone employed in his capacity. We often talked about recipes and methodologies when we were outside having a smoke or taking a break."

Jacques picked up his notebook and flicked back a couple of pages. "I understood that he had no skills to work in a kitchen," he looked up. "Are you now saying the opposite?"

"No, not exactly. At the time that I first knew him he had no professional chef's skills, that's true, which is why he was assigned to wash dishes and pans and other low-grade support tasks. But it was clear to me that he had an aptitude for cooking, and he knew some technicalities which I presumed he had learned from someone in the family. I think it was probably that person who had been professionally trained to some degree. But I don't ever remember him being specific about where he had picked up or acquired his knowledge."

"Alright. So, you met him first in 2000, but what about the period between then and 2009 when he died?"

"We loosely kept in touch. I was in Orléans until the end of the tourist season in 2004, and every so often a postcard would turn up from somewhere else in Europe asking if there was a job. He always included a phone number. If I could use him I would call or text and let him know and then, a couple of weeks or a few days later, he'd turn up. He'd stay for a month or two and then he'd leave."

"And where did he stay when he was working with you?"

Jonnie shrugged. "Wherever he could. Sometimes at my place. Sometimes on the local campsite or with one of the other kitchen staff. Sometimes on the premises."

"And what happened after 2004?"

"I got a better job as a *saucier* in a restaurant in Le Puy-en-Velay, and when a postcard from Beaufort turned up in Orléans, the hotel sent it on to me. Usual thing. I texted him and he turned up in Le Puy shortly afterwards. It was whilst he was in Le Puy that first time that I was able to persuade him to get some formal training. I even paid the majority share of the fees for him."

Jacques looked Jonnie in the eye. "Why? Why would you do that?"

"He had an aptitude for cooking. By then, I'd also realised that he had a nose for putting flavours together, for creating new spice combinations that worked. He had a natural talent, and it would have been a great waste not to enable him to explore that."

"Very magnanimous," said Jacques, his investigator's scepticism rising.

Jonnie sat up straight. "Look! My childhood wasn't very stable or happy, and if a teacher at school hadn't spotted my talent and encouraged me I wouldn't now be working as an executive chef, OK? I wouldn't have three books out, a catering business and an exclusive restaurant franchise. I was repaying the favour by following the example I'd been set."

Jacques absorbed the admonishment and cleared his throat. "OK. What else can you tell me about Antoine?"

"I know he'd spent time in Nepal and Indonesia. That's where I think he may have picked up some of the complex spice combinations that he suggested. We spent some time experimenting with dishes and a couple ended up on the menu that year."

"Did he stay in Le Puy for an extensive period of time then?"

"Not all summer, no. He did some very basic training with a *Chef de Partie* where we were both working at the time and then went to Paris for intensive training in *pâtisserie*. He came back in October, maybe early November, for about a week, I think, and then he disappeared."

"Disappeared? Do you know where?"

Jonnie shook his head. "He never said. Although the holiday season was over, I was still busy with the restaurant and putting together my first book of recipes, and when I did notice he wasn't around, I couldn't find him. Then a postcard arrived from Canada saying he was on his way back to France and that he'd be in touch."

"And was he in touch?"

Jonnie shook his head. "Not until two years later. I'd got my third book in the final stages of preparation for printing; I was *Chef de Cuisine* at Vauclain's place in Montbel. I was also looking for another job because Vauclain wasn't an easy man to get on with. Antoine just walked in and asked for me."

Jacques thought for a moment. "You've not seen or heard from him for two years but he knows where to find you? How is that possible?"

"Vauclain's restaurant was in and out of the local newspapers all the time in 2008 and 2009 and when I arrived in March, so was I by association. It wouldn't have been that difficult for him to find me."

Jacques finished typing up his notes from the day's interviews and filed the documents in the online folders. The blank screen on the desktop challenged him to do more work. Instead, he logged out and turned the monitor off. Casting his eye across his whiteboard, he moved to the other side of the room and updated the notes for the Beaufort case. Returning to his desk, he picked up the phone.

"Didier, can you send someone to the library tomorrow to go through the local papers from 2005 looking for any articles about the restaurant in Montbel, please... Yes... Up to and including any reports about the fire... OK. Thanks... and I'll see you tomorrow."

friday, june 10ᵗʰ

The regular management team meeting completed, Jacques dismissed his people with the exception of Didier Duclos. A tall, lean man with a lived-in face that showed him to have earned every crease and line acquired during his sixty-one years, Didier had come to Vaux Investigations to work as a general office manager and investigator. He had been the first person Jacques had recruited following the internal re-organisation across the whole of the Vaux Group in the first few weeks of 2010. Having worked as a detective in the *Police Nationale* in Mende, Didier had taken early retirement to care for his terminally ill wife. Within the year she had died, and Didier had needed a distraction. It was a chance conversation between Bruno Pelletier and Jacques, shortly following their investigation into the deaths in Merle, that had brought Didier to Jacques' office for an initial exploratory chat some months previously.

"So, what did the library provide for us about the Montbel case?" Jacques pushed his chair back and tossed his pen down on the desk.

"You will get the hang of managing these people, you know."

"Will I? I sometimes wonder." He forced a smile.

"Chef Berger was right. There are numerous articles about the restaurant, the owner, and the staff. But, what I don't understand, and it was something the press picked up on at the time, is why Antoine Beaufort was there on the night of the fire and how he gained access. The restaurant had been closed for three days before the fire occurred." Didier placed a file of papers on the desk in front of Jacques and pulled out three photocopied articles. "These are all asking the same question."

"And that's a question that I've been asking myself," said Jacques as he skimmed the content of the newspaper articles. "When did the media interest in the fire and the death cease?"

"A few weeks later. Once the identity of the body was made public, the journalists moved on to other stories until the conviction became news."

"To be expected. But, if the restaurant was closed for business, then I would have expected any key-holders to have had to return their keys immediately. If that occurred, then how did Beaufort manage to gain access?"

"He didn't hand his keys in or he got another set from someone else… Vauclain or the chef, perhaps?"

"Which may mean that very pat answer I got from Monsieur Vauclain was just that and therefore, he might have known that Beaufort would be there. But what's the connection, Didier? What motive would Vauclain have to make him take the risk of using the fire, something that happened on that particular evening by chance we are told, to remove Beaufort?" Jacques frowned and shook his head. "For me, it doesn't add up."

"I agree. We need to question both Vauclain and Berger again."

"There's something else that's nagging at me. If Beaufort did have keys, where are they? Were they recovered from the scene? Were they damaged as a result of the heat and if so, was there anything in the detailed forensics report to substantiate that? And why? Surely, he would have been paid and laid off on the day of the closure or, at the very latest, the next day. Why was he there, Didier?"

"Yes, I know. That question bothers me too. I'll talk to my old colleagues and see what I can find out."

Jacques glanced at his watch. "Monday. That can wait until Monday." He collected all the papers on his desk together and slotted them into his bag. "Have a good weekend and we'll talk about this case again next week."

**

The afternoon had been very warm, and the evening had become sultry under a heavy sky. In the distance, the indistinct sound of thunder rolled in response to the heat of the day.

"I don't know how you can drink that stuff without ice when it's this warm." Beth sidled out onto the balcony of their apartment in Mende, her slip-on beach sandals snapping on the tiled floor as she walked. Collapsing down on her steamer chair, she cradled a tall glass of lime and soda, clinking with ice, first to one side of her face and then the other.

"It helps me to think, and ice dilutes a good drink." Jacques sipped his single malt whisky and continued to stare ahead. He didn't turn his head or look at her.

Beth reluctantly broke the silence. "You seem very distant tonight, Jacques. Is everything OK?"

He turned to her and smiled. "A new investigation that at first seemed straightforward, but now, there are nothing but unanswered questions. That's why the whisky is necessary," he said holding up the glass and swirling the contents around in front of his eyes.

Beth grinned. "I see. Well, I've something else for us both to think about. I picked up a message today from the estate agent in Leeds. They have an offer on Dan's house."

His interest piqued. "A firm offer?"

"I think so. It's an American businessman who's moving to the UK, so there's no chain. His current property is rented in New York, and he wants to settle as soon as possible."

Jacques swung his legs off his lounger and faced her, his elbows resting on his thighs. "Is it an acceptable offer?"

"It's £10,000 less than the revised asking price."

"So that would be £15,250 less than the market price when you first put the place up for sale, Beth. I know I don't have a detailed understanding of the English housing market, but I think you should negotiate or get the agent to do that for you."

28

"Jacques, there have been only two offers in the last eleven months. The first one fell through, and now this. I'm very tempted to just take it so that I can get rid of the place. It was Dan's place. Now, it's just a constant distraction from what I'm trying to do here." She gazed at the mountainside in the distance as the gradually darkening sky lit up with an ivory striation of lightning. The attendant rumble of thunder following a few moments later.

"But giving the house away doesn't make a lot of sense."

"You're right. But I no longer have any real attachment to the property. I never really did have, if I'm honest. Dan owned it before I married him. Even when I moved in, it still felt like his place... And now. Now that I know he wasn't the man I thought he was, I feel even less attached to the house. I just want to get rid of it. This is where I live. This is where my future is. France. Here with you."

Jacques reached across and took her hand. "Does that mean that we can finally make plans?"

Beth smiled and then looked away. "Do we have to?"

Jacques frowned.

"Make plans, I mean. What's wrong with staying as we are?"

"We can stay as we are if that's what you really want, but it's not what I want, Beth. I'm not Dan. I want us to get married. I would like to have a son and a daughter too, if possible. And, if we can have children, that would make me very happy and...I suppose, complete."

"And what if things don't work out between us?"

Jacques took a deep breath and drained his glass. "That's a risk that we both have to take. We've both made mistakes. We've both made a choice, committed whole-heartedly to someone who wasn't right for each of us. I think, this time I've got it right. I know I have, and my previous mistake means that I know I can make things work for us."

Beth looked at him. There was a sadness in his eyes that she had never seen before. She felt a tightness in the centre of her chest. "I'm not saying never, Jacques. I'm just asking why now?"

"I'm not settled, Beth. My personal life has been a mess for years. As a young detective in Paris, it was exciting, and I had little time to think about family and settling down. Following the shooting, I did a lot of thinking. Perhaps I had too much time to think." The bottle of whiskey was on the floor beside his chair and he poured himself another drink. "That first time I saw you, I knew there was something different about you. I just knew. Then the night of the storm. I knew then I couldn't let you go. But you were...distracted. You were in a difficult place emotionally... And then you left. No explanation. You didn't even say goodbye."

Beth sighed. A streak of orange light spread across the horizon. The almost immediate thunderclap caught her by surprise. She took a deep breath.

"Well, you're right about one thing. I was in a difficult place. Talking to you that night... You made me feel as though I was of importance to you, of interest to you and... Well, it had been such a long time since I'd felt like that."

"So why leave?"

Beth turned to him, tears in her eyes. "The guilt. I'd just buried Dan. I wasn't supposed to feel of importance to anyone. I wasn't supposed to be happy. At the time, I'd just cut and run from everything at home because... I realise now, it was because everything was too damn difficult. Everything had been too difficult for too long and I just couldn't handle it anymore. I never told anyone at home where I was going. Not mum. Not dad. Not even my neighbour across the road who looked after the house whenever we were away. I just packed a bag and got on a train."

A sudden rush of cold wind with the promise of ice on its tail swept across the balcony, and Beth closed her eyes in the momentary relief of the unexpected coolness.

"You once told me that us being together was a mistake."

She winced at his reminder, and for a fleeting moment she was back on the porch, tears in her eyes, watching him striding away from her and towards the gate. "That was then, Jacques. Now is different, and I was wrong. So very wrong when I said that."

"Good," he said, a broad smile spreading across his face for the first time since arriving home.

Beth grinned. "Let me get the house finalised. I'll contact the agent and agree the price first thing tomorrow morning. Then, in about a month, maybe six week's time everything should be settled. Maybe then we can make plans."

"That will be towards the end of July," said Jacques after counting the dates on his fingers. "Papa, Francis, Thérèse, and the boys will be here in August. What do you think?"

"August? A wedding in August?" She heard the tremor in her own voice as she uttered the words. "I... Umm... It's so soon. So very soon"

"Or September, or October?"

"Let's just finalise the house and then we'll decide."

A searing orange and yellow light illuminated the broad smile on Jacques' face as the sky cracked overhead. He looked up. A final rush of freezing wind, and Jacques was on his feet.

"Quickly," he said. "A storm is on the way. Get inside and pull the windows across."

Unsure what the real problem was, Beth just moved as instructed. Jacques removed the cushions from the chairs and moved inside to help with the windows. The first hailstone landed at Beth's feet. It was about half the size of a golf ball. She bent to pick it up.

"What the...?"

The sky roared. Jacques battled to secure the final window as a white shower descended. Safe inside, they both watched as the wind lashed the windows with balls of ice. Within twenty minutes the whole of the balcony was covered in a thick layer of gleaming hail. The sky, alternately orange and yellow and pink continued to rage above them.

Jacques moved across to Beth and put his arm around her. "It's all right," he said. "We're safe, but I just hope your car is in the underground car park and not in the courtyard."

Beth took a few moments to process his comment, her attention so intent on weather she had never experienced before.

"Underground car park." She nestled her head against his warm chest.

saturday, june 11ᵗʰ

The door to Marie Mancelle's house, in the village of Messandrierre, was wide open. Inside, the honeyed tones of a mellow tenor voice were drifting out onto the main street. Beth hesitated at the entrance to the small garden. *Martin is home. Perhaps I shouldn't interrupt.* She turned, intending to take her invitations to the rest of the village and come back later, but Pierre ran out.

"Bonjour, Madame Elizabeth," he shouted. "*Maman* says the picture of me for your studio will be ready soon. When can I see it?"

Beth smiled as she realised how much taller he had grown over the last few months. Although the chubbiness of childhood had gone, he was still small for his age. His once round face seemed thinner, but his thick dark hair was all over the place as usual.

"You can see it any time you like, Pierre; perhaps Monday after school?"

The boy pulled a face. "I have my music lesson on Monday after school."

"OK. Well, Tuesday or Wednesday, then. But…I have your parent's invitation to the opening of the shop and studio on Thursday," she said, holding up the envelope addressed to them. "I was hoping that you would want to come as well. You can see it then if one of the other days isn't convenient." She offered him the envelope, but he didn't take it.

"OK. Come in," he said, dashing a short way back into the house. "*Maman*," he shouted through an open doorway. "You have a visitor. It's Madame Elizabeth." Turning to Beth, "It's OK. Just go in. And don't mind the noise, *Papa*'s

33

just practicing for a new role. I'm going to the *gendarmerie, Maman.*" One last beaming smile to Beth, and he ran off down the street.

Hesitating on the doorstep, Beth watched him as he disappeared through the houses.

"Beth! Come in, please." Marie ushered her into the spacious living room that stretched the full-length of the old farmhouse and occupied one half of the property downstairs.

"I don't want to interrupt, Marie. I realise that Martin's home and Pierre's told me he's working. I just wanted to invite you both and Pierre to the opening of the studio, that's all." She handed over the invitation.

"Of course, we'll all be there," Marie said, ripping open the envelope. "And you are not interrupting. I've told Martin to make some coffee, and he will be here in a few moments. Please, sit down." She scraped the morning paper off one end of the large cream coloured sofa and settled herself.

Beth sat on the opposite side of the corner settee. "Thanks, and there's something else that I would like to ask."

Marie nodded and smiled.

"Jacques and I have been talking, and now that the property in England is about to be sold... Well, Jacques wants me to start planning a wedding. Umm, our wedding, that is. We've no definite date yet. That will depend on how the sale goes and when it completes. But...perhaps August or September might be a good time, and I was hoping that you both would be here so that you could attend. Maybe Pierre could take a role? I don't know. I was also wondering if, perhaps either you or Martin would help me with the music, possibly even—"

"The answer's yes," interrupted Marie as she skirted the coffee table to give Beth a hug. "I'm so pleased for you both."

Martin, poised and carrying a tray ladened with cups, saucers and biscuits, halted in the doorway. "Does this mean congratulations are in order?"

Before Beth could answer, Marie had moved across the room and had taken the tray without pausing for breath. "In a couple of months, Martin. They are getting married at the end of summer, and we are providing the music, and I've already said that you will sing. We haven't had chance to decide which pieces, but I was thinking that *Mon coeur s'ouvre à ta voix* might be a good choice, or perhaps something from *Manon,* and what about the beginning of *Au fond du temple saint* through to the chorus or there is also that song from the Italian film that you often sing, the one that I can never remember the name of, or there's—"

"Marie, Marie. I would need a baritone for *Au fond,* so slow down and let Beth decide."

Beth smiled at Martin, grateful for the opportunity to take control of the conversation again. "I just wanted to pose the idea to you today, Marie, before I made the suggestion to Jacques. And the idea only occurred to me as I arrived here and heard your beautiful singing, Martin. I just wanted to ask for your help with choosing the music, that was all." She watched as the bright smile on Marie's face slipped away to be replaced by embarrassment and finally genuine contrition.

"I'm getting carried away. I'm so sorry, Beth, please forgive me, but I am just so happy for the both of you, and we will help in any way that we can. Now, let's have coffee and talk through some ideas, shall we?" She began setting out the cups and saucers on the table. She glanced at her husband. "Martin, the coffee? Milk and sugar too, please?"

"Of course," he said as he disappeared from the room.

***

"*Gendarme* Mancelle reporting for duty!" Pierre burst through the open door of the *gendarmerie* and ducked under the counter to join Jacques and *Gendarme* Thibault Clergue in the cramped office space.

"No salute today, Pierre?" Jacques, perched on the corner

of the desk, a stern look on his face but a smile in his eyes, waited for a response. The boy frowned and then burst into laughter.

"I know you're joking, Monsieur Jacques."

"Good. As a detective you have to be able to read people's faces accurately. *Gendarme* Clergue tells me you're working on a couple of cases together."

"Yes. We're looking for some graffiti artists and some poachers." The brightness in his eyes faded as a frown covered his face, "We found a badger in a trap last week," he continued. "The vet couldn't save the animal and had to put it down."

Jacques cast a questioning glance at Thibault who shrugged as his response.

"Jacques and I have some business to complete, Pierre, do your parents know where you are?"

The boy nodded.

"And have you got your new phone with you?"

Another nod.

"To work, then, and I'll catch up with you in a moment." As soon as Pierre was gone, Clergue got up from his desk. "I know what you're thinking, and you're right," he said. "But, I couldn't do it. Not in front of the boy. When you and Beth have children of your own you'll realise that, as much as you want them to survive in this difficult world, you also want to protect them from some of the harsh realities for as long as you possibly can. It's a parent's constant dilemma." He collected the keys from the desk drawer and moved to the door. "We can talk whilst I keep an eye on Pierre, but I need to catch up with him or he'll be in the woods all by himself."

Clergue locked the door and the two men marched along the road, past the restaurant and up the hill towards the lake, quickly shortening the 150-metre lead the boy had created.

"Is Fabien going to charge the municipality for the consultation about the badger?"

Clergue grinned. "No, I've managed it. I telephoned Pierre's grandfather and *Maire* Mancelle said he would cover the cost himself. But, in the end, Fabien didn't send a bill."

Jacques nodded. "Good. The fire at the restaurant in Montbel, Thibault, you were saying something about Vauclain before Pierre arrived."

"I wasn't involved in that case, Jacques, but, as you know, in a village like this you hear things and I've been led to believe that Vauclain was a difficult man. Did you know he refused to pay his bills at the *boulangerie* in Rieutort for almost 3 months? Madame Mancelle even got involved on her sister-in-law's behalf. I remember being told she went to the restaurant, and she and Vauclain had a stand-up argument in front of a roomful of diners."

"Is it the blue trail today?" shouted Pierre as he stood at the entrance to one of the managed routes through the forest.

"No, we're taking the logging route to start with."

Pierre turned on his heel and started to jog further up the incline and past the junction by the dead oak.

"Unpaid bills, that could suggest anything from a temporary cash flow problem to a serious debt."

Thibault nodded. "I think it may have been a bit more than cash flow. A few months after that *Boucher* Laval in Langogne employed a private debt collector, a local heavy and known criminal, as it turned out, to put the frighteners on Vauclain."

"And the outcome?"

"Vauclain on the phone to the *gendarmerie* alleging assault, but it came to nothing. One thing I did notice, when I went to see the man about something else, the staff in that place were not happy. A couple of the women waiting tables were openly hostile about, and towards, Vauclain."

"And what about Antoine Beaufort? Is there anything you can tell me about him?"

Clergue stopped a few metres short of where Pierre was sat on a low boulder that signalled the entrance to the logging route. Not that it needed any form of annunciation. The earth and rubble of the rough track had long been gouged into deep ruts by the tyres of the ladened trucks.

"Not really. He did use the campsite here for a short time, and Gaston can tell you more. He seemed to be very friendly with the chef, though. I remember them being deep in conversation at the side of the building when I called."

"And when was this?"

"Just before the fire, I think. I can't remember the precise date, but it will be on record. Very beginning of July, probably. Pelletier had you working on the Sithrez murders at the time."

Jacques' face clouded at the mention of the name. "That's a case I don't want to revisit," he said. "Thanks, Thibault. I'll get Gaston to check his records and take it from there."

***

Across the village, the morning was being used by Delacroix to catch up on his investments and to chat to his associates around the globe in his completed office space. Business finished for the day, he glanced at the oil painting that he'd fixed to the wall earlier in the week and smiled. He shut down the computer. He had a more pressing task to undertake. A task that had thwarted him since he first walked into the place on Tuesday November 3rd, 2009. He recoiled at the remembered sight and smell of the place as it had been then.

Over the months in between when he had been required in the village, his attention had been focussed on getting the place habitable and remodelled to his needs. All the rubbish that he'd found, Guy Delacroix's personal papers, boxes of stuff that had been stashed in the attic, reams of old newspapers and bundles of old clothes, the detritus of another man's life, had gradually been disposed of. Now, he was left with just the four boxes he'd found in the attic, two large suitcases, and the locked trunk.

"There has to be something in these," he said to himself as he dragged a couple of the boxes out of the *cave* and into his office space. Making himself comfy in one of the chairs at the large oval table, he pulled open the nearest box. The dust made him sneeze, and the old newspaper covering the top of the contents almost disintegrated in his hands as he lifted it out.

Still sneezing, he got up and pushed open the two lights that sat high in the wall of the cellar behind him. Returning to the *cave*, he pulled a roll of bin bags from the bottom drawer of the cabinet next to the small sink and detached a number of them. He was sure he would need them.

Back in his office, he decided he needed to clarify exactly what it was that he was looking for. Collecting his mobile from his desk, he dialled a number in Canada.

"Hi... Yeah, I'm fine thanks... Was back last month for a couple of weeks... Yeah, the place is finished now, and I got back here last week. Now I'm staying for as long it suits... You got that right. Look, I just want to know exactly what it is I'm looking for... Hang on."

He grabbed a note pad from his desk drawer and began jotting down a list as he repeated what he was hearing. "Title deeds, OK... Will? Are you sure about that? OK... Letters, OK... Certificates, accounts and... No, considering the state of the place when I first arrived I don't think there will be... OK. Yeah... Sure, I'll get back to you." He ended the call and scanned the list.

As he sorted through the papers, he put those of interest on the table and the rest went straight into one of the bags. About halfway down the box, he came across an oblong metal tin that looked as though it had once contained sweets of some sort. When he grabbed it to lift it out he realised it was much heavier than he anticipated.

"OK. What do we have here?" He placed the tin in the centre of a couple of sheets of old newspaper from the box. He carefully prised the lid open and his eyes widened in surprise.

"Guy, you old skinflint." He grabbed his phone intending to dial his contact in Canada. But as he scrolled through his contacts list, he stopped and thought better of it. "Better wait and see what we really have here." He put the phone down and ran his fingers through the hundreds and hundreds of coins in the box. He grabbed a handful and spread them out in front of him. He started moving them around, the silver to one side, the copper and other metals to individual piles of their own. Beginning with the silver, he put them into some sort of order. All the old French coins together on his left, those from elsewhere in the world in separate piles on his right. Recognising an old American coin, he examined it closely.

"I think there maybe something here," he said as a wide smile spread across his face.

He continued searching through the box and brigading the coins for almost an hour. Satisfied that he'd seen enough, he stopped and dialled on his computer to a number in Morocco. As he waited for his Internet call to be answered he adjusted his thinking to Arabic. It had been a while since he had last needed to use this particular and complex language. As the handsome but inscrutable face of his long-time business associate in Rabat came onto the screen, Delacroix smiled and greeted him respectfully. He knew he had to use the right approach with Hakim, otherwise everything could be lost.

"Hakim, I have something that I am sure will be of especial interest to you, my friend," he said, his tone business-like but soft. He made sure that his usual North American brashness was kept at bay. That well-rehearsed and staged brashness was useful for his associates in Canada and the annoying neighbours in the village, but it would never, ever do for Hakim.

Delacroix sorted through the other three boxes and found very little of interest or value. He then spent the whole afternoon gradually working through the coins, listing them, noting their condition, date, and country of origin as Hakim had suggested. He also added in anything else that he thought might be useful. He glanced at his watch. It was 19.10 and he needed to eat. The coins he'd listed had gone straight back into the box. He gathered up the remainder and dropped them into a large envelope and locked everything in his safe.

Remembering he'd promised to keep in touch with his associate in Canada, he grabbed his phone and dialled. He braced himself ready for the conversation.

"Hey, hi there, it's me again... Our little business agreement, it's not going so well... I thought I'd finally got something... Yeah, I know... Well, I was hoping all those hours of looking and searching might finally be about to pay off... But still nothing... No there are still some suitcases to sort through and a trunk... OK. I'll keep in touch."

He ended the call and grinned to himself as he recalled what Hakim had said. 'Coins do have a value, you know, you just need to know what you are looking for.'

Yes, Hakim, he thought. *Coins do have a value, and I will also be taking my list to someone else here in France.* He may not know much about coin collecting, but he knew enough to always be prepared for any possible business deal, and, to Delacroix, that always meant being one or two steps ahead of whoever he was dealing with at any one time.

His stomach registered yet another complaint and he thought about taking dinner in the village restaurant, but decided against it. He strolled across to his *cave* and picked out an expensive bottle of Burgundy. He knew it could be a little premature, but nevertheless, he felt like celebrating.

sunday, june 12th

Beth checked the data from the spreadsheet against the table she had up on screen. *This isn't the right way to present this.* She blew out her cheeks in frustration but saved the presentation as it was anyway. Picking up the document Jacques had given her, she folded the sheet of paper so that she could see only the final results: the month by month costs for the previous twelve-month period directly contrasted with the twelve month period ending in May for his work area within the Vaux Group. Working through each pair of figures she subtracted one from the other and jotted down the difference. Halfway through the data she stopped and looked at the results.

"Got it!" She said to herself. Moving through the presentation swiftly, she deleted the last few slides and replaced them with one single pictorial, added a heading and a comment at the foot. A spell-check and a cross-check for consistency, and the task Jacques had asked her to undertake would be complete. She saved the presentation for the last time then, sitting back in her chair, she gazed out of the loft window and across the rugged landscape to Mont Lozère. Below in the snug, she could hear the muffled sounds of Jacques as he fixed the series of newly framed photographs that she had taken to the wall.

Running her hand across the sheet of glass inset into the small ivory painted table that now served as her desk, she smiled with satisfaction at the changes she'd made. The old-fashioned dark wood and metal desk that had been there before was gone. The dark stained wooden floors throughout the chalet had been sanded and lightened to a pale grey that toned with one of the flecks in the stone used for the fireplaces and the feature walls in the main living space. The remaining wooden walls had been skimmed and plastered and painted ivory. The heavy brown leather furniture that her deceased husband had favoured was now replaced by more modern items that were pine framed and the whole place seemed to Beth much lighter and more airy. The spiral staircase had also been revitalised, the ironwork frame was now painted ivory and the wooden slats had been sanded and stained the same colour as the floors. The loft area with its deep maroon sofas and glass coffee table was the place she liked to be in summer. The snug was for winter.

"What are you grinning at?" Jacques looked across at her as he reached the top of the stairs.

"My handiwork!" She stretched and yawned. "I know getting this place re-vamped took me a lot of time and a lot of money for the English guys who did most of the work, but I am really pleased with how the place looks now. And I still say this is the best place for my occasional table-cum-desk. I know you don't agree, but it is."

Jacques laughed. "If arguing about where a table goes is the worst thing that happens to us then I think we will be happy. Come and see the snug now that I've fixed your pictures to the wall." He turned and ran down the stairs. Beth followed quickly afterwards.

"Your presentation for your meeting tomorrow is all done, too. I need to take you through it, though because I found a better way of presenting the data. And you really must try and understand how this software works, Jacques." At the bottom of the stairs, she stopped. Jacques was barring her way.

"In that case, you need to learn how to use a power drill," he said, a wide grin on his face.

***

Delacroix had spent the morning completing the list of coins, which he had emailed to his associate, Hakim, in

Rabat. He wasn't expecting a response for at least a month. There was a lot to look at and check, and his associate was not known for his speed in handling business. Everything would be done, according to Hakim, when 'the time was right'. Pushing the previous day's find to the back of his mind, he decided he would take at look at what was in the old leather suitcases.

It took all his strength to carry both of them together out of the *cave* and into the light and airiness of his workspace. Setting the first one carefully on a cloth on the table, he examined it. The leather was dry; the metal catches were rusted and were of a design that had not been used for over forty years. *These must have been expensive when they were first bought.* He ran a cloth over the surface and that was when he noticed the name on the front in gold lettering, 'C. Vauquelin'. He repeated the surname to himself several times, just to see how it felt and sounded.

"Yeah, sounds good," he said as he went to fetch his toolbox. "And, one thing's for sure, Ricky, you never know when you might need another name."

Selecting a chisel, he began to prise the locks and they gave way in moments. He pulled up the lid. There was tissue paper laid across the top of the contents and he pulled it aside. Underneath were women's clothes. He lifted a few items out, making sure they maintained their carefully folded shapes, and placed them on the glass. He searched a little deeper. The case was full of clothing. He lifted out a pale blue blouse and shook it out.

"Wow! Clémence Delacroix *née* Vauquelin, you sure knew quality when you saw it." The blouse was small in his hands. "And I'm guessing your figure was *petite*." He started pulling out other items. There was underwear, stockings, skirts, beautiful summer dresses, more blouses, cardigans, and sleeveless fine knitted tops. Everything a woman might have brought with her into a new marriage.

He moved onto the second case and, leaving it where it was on the floor, prised the locks open. This case was full of coats, jackets and heavier skirts, tops and dresses. Again all of it of the same quality as the lighter items spread all over the table.

Delacroix slumped down in his chair. "A whole wardrobe!" He ran his hands through his hair. "What the hell do I do with that?"

He cast his eyes across the room and the clothing. To him, everything had to have a value. Preferably a monetary value, but, if all that was available was the improvement of his standing or a good dose of kudos, he would accept that too. But a wardrobe of female clothing was another matter. He had no idea of whether there was value in what he was looking at or not. He drummed his fingers on the only spare piece of tabletop within easy reach.

Unable to make a decision, he got up and poured himself a beer from the fridge in the *cave*. Circling the table, he gazed at the array of clothes.

"Would anyone be interested in this stuff?" A thought occurred to him and a smile crossed his face. He moved to his desk and picked up the invitation to Beth's opening that was propped up against the monitor.

"Want to know what to do with female clothing? Ask a woman, of course!" He finished his beer and began to refold and pack the clothes. He would get some coat hangers when he was next in Mende. And that, he thought to himself, will be the afternoon of the opening.

The clothing all dealt with and re-packed, he decided he would try to open the trunk. He pulled it away from the wall. Settled on the floor, he examined it thoroughly. The large single lock was rusted shut and, despite his attempts to free it, remained resolutely unmoved. Twisting himself round to look at the back, he scrutinised the hinges. These were also rusted but he thought it might be possible to remove the pins from each one if necessary. Turning his attention to the front again, he decided he would try the lock first.

Using a chisel and a hammer, he gradually worked away at the lock until it sheared off the trunk. With the mechanism broken, it took only a few minutes to remove the remaining pieces and free the flange. He undid the buckles on the straps either side and lifted the lid.

The inside of the trunk looked in pristine condition. The *moiré* silk lining of the lid had retained its deep red colour and the contents were all wrapped in white tissue paper. Delacroix stood.

"What do we have here? More clothes, maybe?" The neatness of the presentation made him look at his grubby hands. "These won't do, Ricky," he said as he disappeared into the *cave* to rinse them under the tap.

He wiped his hands and returned to the trunk. Gingerly, he lifted out the topmost package. It was small and very light. He placed it carefully on the table and peeled back the tissue paper. Inside, he found a tiny pair of white knitted bootees with fine pink silk ribbon at the ankles. The next, slightly larger parcel revealed a tiny little coat, knitted in the same intricate pattern with the same ribbon at the bodice. He continued to lift out the packets of tissue paper. As he gradually worked his way through the contents of the trunk he realised that what had been preserved was a baby's layette. On the table was every item that a newborn child would need. However, unlike the things he'd seen in stores in Québec or advertised on TV, these were all hand-made and had an old-fashioned look to his eyes.

"Why would..." He let his question drift. He needed to think. If there really was a child, that could ruin all his plans. He considered the colour of the ribbon.

"What if she's still alive?"

He was about to pick up his phone and call Canada again, but hesitated. What would he say? What exactly did he know at the moment? He persuaded himself that all he had found was a set of child's clothing. So far, he had no definite information about the owner of that clothing. And that, he decided was what he needed more than anything else, information. This find, like the coins, would remain his find alone until he knew exactly what he was dealing with. In the meantime he had the rest of the trunk to search through and empty. He spent the next couple of hours sorting through what remained. Papers of any interest he put to one side and the rest he threw in one of the bin bags. His first task the next day would be to start working through all the papers and documents he had retained and undertaking some serious research, beginning with the family grave. He paused and thought for a moment. A visit to the family grave.

To make that look right to the rest of the village, I'll need flowers.

He revised his agenda for the week. *A trip to Mende tomorrow as well as Thursday.*

monday, june 13th

Didier parked on Grande Rue in Montbel and followed Jacques to the front door of Étienne Vauclain's house. He knocked but there was no reply.

"He does know we're coming here today, doesn't he?"

Jacques nodded. "I phoned him on his mobile and left a message as soon as I got home on Friday."

Didier knocked again, and after a few moments he moved away and down the side of the property to peer through a window.

"I don't like the look of this, Jacques. It's a bright summer's morning and all the lights are on, and I can see what looks like a mobile phone on the floor."

Instinctively, Jacques tried the front door. "This is locked. See if you can get in through the French windows," he said as he moved in the opposite direction and around the side of the property looking for another means of access. As he came full circle, he found Didier standing in front of the open French windows.

They both stepped into the room. "Monsieur Vauclain, it's Jacques Forêt. I called on Friday to let you know I would be here today." He paused. "Monsieur Vauclain?" He listened and after a few moments of complete silence he carefully placed his bag on the floor by the open window.

"We need to find Vauclain. You take upstairs and the gallery and I'll cover this floor." Jacques moved towards the sofas arranged around the fireplace on his right. The grate was clean and looked as though it had not been lit for a while. Making his way to the other side of the living space, he briefly stopped at the computer desk and glanced at the open laptop surrounded by papers. In the kitchen and dining area there were the remnants of some whisky in a glass on the draining board. The door of the dishwasher was ajar. Teasing it further open, he noticed that it was empty, but the chef's block of knives on the worktop above caught his interest.

"There's no-one upstairs," said Didier as he crossed the living space to the kitchen.

"There's a knife missing." Stepping forward Jacques made his way to a door in the corner. He kicked the draft excluder away and a faint sour smell seeped into the kitchen. He hesitated for a moment and then turned the keys that were already in the lock. As he opened the door, the heavy metallic smell of dried blood flooded the room. He'd never got used to that particular odour. Holding his handkerchief across his nose and mouth, he stepped into the garage. On his right on the wall he found a light switch. He stepped further into the space. On the far side, between the car and the opposite wall, he found what he knew would be there. Pinching his handkerchief tightly around his nose, he looked away. His stomach gave a flip and he took a step back. As he re-entered the kitchen he took a gulp of air.

"It's Vauclain," he said. "Slit throat. I expect he bled out and has probably been there all weekend. Call it in, Didier. And make sure you speak to Pelletier."

As his colleague made the call, Jacques swiftly returned to his bag and took out two pairs of evidence gloves. He left a set on the kitchen worktop for Didier and pulled on the second pair. Half-listening to the report being made, he strode across the living space and retrieved the mobile phone. A click of the button on the side and it came to life. *A password screen, damn.* He tried an obvious combination of numbers and, at the third attempt, 2222 cleared the screen. Navigating backwards through the call history, he found the record of his own call on Friday evening and the even earlier call that preceded his last visit on Thursday. Taking his business phone from his jacket pocket he took some photographs of Vauclain's call history as he moved forward again through each page to the most recent contact.

Carefully replacing the phone where he had found it, he moved to the coffee table and swiftly searched through the journals and papers that were scattered there. The mantelpiece was the next place of interest, but it yielded nothing more enlightening than an old dog-eared postcard from Cannes, a box of matches, and a bill. He checked the back of the postcard and then captured a photograph of it on his phone.

"They're on their way, and Pelletier will be here in about twenty minutes," said Didier as he pulled on his gloves and moved to the desk.

Jacques joined him and began a search of the papers. "Try and access the laptop. He might have used the same password as on the phone. It's double two, double two." Jacques watched as Didier keyed in the numbers. It didn't work.

"Damn it. And there doesn't seem to be anything amongst this lot, either."

"These might be useful," said Didier as he leafed through some papers enclosed in a notebook. Holding the papers upright to show what was lying beneath, Jacques nodded and took photographs of each sheet.

"Bank statements. They could be very useful. Anything else?"

Didier shook his head and replaced everything exactly as it had been.

"Let's get out of here. This is a crime scene now." Pulling off his gloves, Jacques collected his bag and moved out onto the patio to await the arrival of the police.

Pelletier pulled up outside the house as the detectives and pathologists took responsibility for the crime scene. He made his way towards Jacques and Didier.

"So, what have we got?" Standing at the entrance of the French windows, the investigating magistrate meticulously took in the scene.

Jacques referred to his notebook. "Male, I can identify him as Étienne Vauclain. Throat cut. There is a knife missing from the chef's block in the kitchen, which I've assumed to be the murder weapon. The body was found on the floor in the garage, which I accessed through the door on the far left in the kitchen. That door was locked on the inside when we arrived."

"And your reason for being here?"

"To interview Vauclain about Antoine Beaufort for my client. I spoke to him last on Thursday."

"Anything else I should know?"

"Other than opening the door to the garage and, after checking the perimeter of the property and gaining access through the French windows, everything is exactly as we found it. We entered the property because we saw the phone on the floor and noticed that all the lights were on. We both thought entry was justified." He decided to keep everything else to himself.

"Was Vauclain expecting you?"

"Yes. I telephoned him on Friday evening at around 18.30 and left a message on his voicemail."

Pelletier nodded. "Thanks Jacques, leave this to me, but we'll need formal statements from you both." he said.

***

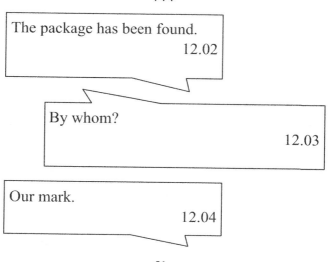

> The package has been found.
> 12.02

> By whom?
> 12.03

> Our mark.
> 12.04

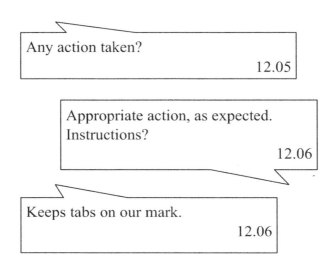

Any action taken?

12.05

Appropriate action, as expected.
Instructions?

12.06

Keeps tabs on our mark.

12.06

***

Dumping his bag on his desk, Jacques slumped down in his chair and stared at the whiteboard opposite.

"A key witness murdered, Didier," he said and let out a world-weary sigh. "Vauclain had more to tell us, I'm certain of that, and if we had leaned on him, we might have got at half of the truth. Whether we will ever get that missing information now…I doubt it."

"We still have the information we've picked up today."

"Yes, but I don't see how it can help us with the investigation into Beaufort's life prior to 2009. But we will follow up on it." He pulled his phone out and scrolled through to the photo album for the day. "Download all of these and check each number and get the bank statements uploaded into the network file. There was a phone number on the back of the postcard as well. Can we get that checked too, please?"

Didier nodded and took the phone. "I'll use this for the calls to each of the numbers we need to check, and then I'll return it to the IT people for another SIM and number to be allocated."

"Good idea, and ask IT to set up another phone immediately for me, please, with the usual contacts list." Before he reached the office door, Jacques stopped Didier with another request. "And let me know as soon as the bank statements are online. I have a question at the back of mind that I need to exorcise."

"Of course." A moment later he was gone.

Left alone, Jacques stared at his whiteboard his mind reeling at the outcome of the visit to Vauclain. Refusing to be stymied by the setback, he marched to the board and started adding notes in the column marked 'ACTIONS'.

The *château* and the Beaufort family estate nestled in a valley to the south east of Le Puy-en-Velay. The formal gardens to the side of the house and the long herbaceous border that flanked the straight drive were in full bloom. The taxi pulled up at the front of the property.

"Put the fare on the account, please," said Jacques as he got out. The four steps to the paved terrace were wide and ran the full length of the frontage. As he approached the door, he saw someone inside who moved forward and opened it.

"Monsieur Forêt?"

Jacques nodded.

"Madame Beaufort is in her sitting room on the first floor. Follow me, please." With that, the man turned and strode across the wide hallway and up the stairs to a large room at the front of the house.

Henriette Beaufort was painfully thin and drawn. Her white hair was neatly coiffed, and her clothes were expensive, classically timeless and engulfed her tiny, withered frame. Manœuvring her electric wheelchair a little closer to the coffee table, she indicated the sofa opposite for Jacques to sit.

"Madame Beaufort, thank you for agreeing to see me today." Resting his bag on the seat beside him, he removed a slim file of papers.

"Monsieur Forêt." She inclined her head slightly as a formal greeting. "I hope that you have good news for me."

"Unfortunately not, Madame." Jacques decided that a direct approach would be appropriate. "I believe that your son is dead," he continued, keeping his tone quiet and calm, "and that he died in a fire in the village of Montbel two years ago. This is a copy of the death certificate, there is an autopsy report, and there are witness statements to support this contention from which I have collated the relevant information." He laid a neatly typed report out on the coffee table in front of her. "I have interviewed two key witnesses myself, and all the evidence suggests to me that the man who died in the fire in the restaurant in Montbel was your son."

"You are wrong, Monsieur. All the evidence that I have suggests to me that he is alive."

The strength and depth in her voice made Jacques wince. He thumbed through his papers as a momentary distraction from the sharpness and clarity of the look in her hazel eyes.

"This morning when you telephoned," she added, "you informed my assistant that you had some questions about the death, and now you are here telling me my son is dead and that there the matter ends. What is this, Monsieur?"

"It is not the death that I am questioning. It is the reason why your son was in that location at the time of his death. And until I can get some clarity on that issue, it is almost impossible for me to say whether any other questions arise. But I am certain that your son is dead."

Madame Beaufort snorted her disapproval. "Nonsense!" She delivered her last statement with such force that she needed to take a couple of gulps of air from the small oxygen tank attached to the back of her chair. Her breathing still uneven, she remained silent and still for a few moments.

"Madame, other than the one outstanding question that I have, I'm very reluctant to look further into this case because the evidence, to me, seems compelling. Unless there is some new evidence that has arisen recently, or you are aware of something that did not come out in the original investigation, then I can see no reason to continue. I am also obliged to inform you that, if there is some completely new evidence that was never considered at the time of the death, I may not be able to do any further work because the original investigation may need to be officially re-opened." Jacques waited as he endured his client's unnerving and lengthy stare, mentally refusing to allow himself to show any sign of discomfort.

"Would you please fetch the open book from my desk over there?"

Jacques complied and as he returned to his seat, he flicked through a few of the pages. "A recipe book, Madame Beaufort? What has that to do with the death of your son?"

Henriette remained silent until he had taken his seat again. "There are a number of pages that have been marked."

Jacques turned to a page separated from its counterpart by a thin slip of paper and read the words that had been highlighted towards the top. He noted that one of the ingredients in the recipe had also been highlighted. He leafed through until he found the other pages and again read the highlighted words.

"I don't understand," he said as he placed the open book on the table in front of him.

"Only my son would know about that combination of spices on page 128. It was my mother's favourite recipe. Only my son would refer to himself in the introduction to the recipe on page 33 by the nickname his great-grandmother gave to me, and which I then gave to him, it's *Breton*. And the comment at the bottom of the recipe on page 78, only my son would know that because I used to say that to him when he was a boy. Again, it is a *Breton* expression."

Jacques looked at the front cover. The title, *Recettes de Ma Petite Cuisine Cévenole,* detailed in large dark blue letters on a white ground, sat in a silver-edged box. Below that was the photograph of a smiling chef in his kitchen surrounded by ingredients, as though he were partway through his preparation for a dish. At the bottom, in the same script but slightly smaller and surrounded by another silver-edged box, was the word *Hiver*. Opening the cover again, he turned to the copyright page.

"This was published in December 2010 but the photograph on the cover is not of your son. It's of a chef named Jonnie Berger. He is one of the witnesses that I have already interviewed. He knew your son and he worked with him. By all appearances they were quite friendly and remained in contact with each other for a number of years. Isn't it possible that Chef Berger and your son swapped recipes? Chef Berger has already explained to me that he and Antoine would talk about spicing, and that some of your son's ideas for dishes were added to the restaurant menu where they were both working at the time."

"I didn't know that," she said, fingering the string of pearls at her neck. Her breathing had become laboured again and she reached for her oxygen mask and took a few gulps of air. A little colour gradually returned to her ashen cheeks.

"I didn't know," she said, her voice as strong as before. "But I do know that my son, and only my son, could have been the source for the information I have pointed out to you." Her face set, she stared at Jacques. The momentary silence was shattered by the metallic clunk of the large brass door handle as Madame's assistant wheeled in a trolley ladened with tea. Bringing it to a halt, he transferred everything to the low table.

"Thank you. I'll pour myself," she said. Her assistant nodded and left. As Henriette busied herself with the tea, Jacques took a few moments to properly take in his surroundings. Accepting the drink, he noticed that the old fashioned and predominantly green pattern on the china was at odds with the equally antiquated pink and white floral wallpaper of the room. Everything about the room, the *décor,* the furnishings, and the carpet suggested old money.

Like the entrance hall and the stairway, the room had an air of careful but well-worn use.

"Madame Beaufort, there are some things that I would like to talk to you about, but I think you may find the conversation difficult, possibly upsetting."

"Henriette. Please call me Henriette," she said taking a sip of her tea. "I may be in a wheelchair, Monsieur, but mentally I'm very strong. I've always had to be, ever since I was a girl."

Jacques acknowledged her fortitude with a half-smile. "From my interview with Chef Berger, I know that your son had been working in Le Puy a few years ago."

Henriette stared at him, her cup halfway to her mouth. "When?" She stammered out the word again. "When? When was this?" She replaced her tea on the table and then wiped a tear from her right eye.

"He was there from 2005 for quite a while." Jacques looked at her. Her normally pale skin was grey, a frown creased her forehead and her eyes were blinking back more tears.

"And he never once came to see me." Her voice was quiet, and hoarse with emotion. "Not once."

Jacques let her think his revelation through for a few seconds longer.

"Henriette, when Antoine was a boy, what would you have said were his strengths? His best aptitudes?"

"He liked puzzles. When he was three, four and five he would take all his Christmas presents apart. He always wanted to know how things worked. All his toy vehicles were always dismantled and then rebuilt. We thought he was destined to be an engineer or perhaps an architect. When he was six, we employed a new nanny for him and his older brother. She was a fabulous cook and it was then that he became interested in baking and cooking. He wanted to know everything and when she was in the kitchen making the children their meals, Antoine was always there too. Between them, they invented the *Tarte au Beaufort*. It was a favourite dish for years and still is." Henriette smiled at the memory. "That's why I am certain he is still alive. Look at page 227. That's *Tarte au Beaufort*. To the very last ingredient that is our dessert. And yes, your chef may have made it as individual *tartelettes* rather than the large one that we still serve here, and he may have been more extravagant with the accompaniments and the decoration, but that is our recipe. Only Antoine and his nanny would know that recipe."

"Did it ever occur to you that he might want to make himself a career in catering, either when he was a small child or later?"

Henriette shrugged. "No, I thought it was a childish phase and that he would move onto something else once he got bored or the nanny left. My husband actively encouraged him to think about other, more useful and more masculine pursuits."

"More masculine? My understanding is that the majority of chefs are men."

"Perhaps, but that wasn't how Charles saw it. It was working in a kitchen. To him it was menial. He had very fixed ideas for both of the boys. Jean-Charles, my eldest, would take over the running of the business and the estate, and Antoine would enter a profession – the law or accountancy. Something 'clean', as Charles would say, and 'respectable'."

"The photo in the frame on your desk, Madame. May I take a closer look?"

Henriette nodded. Jacques picked up the picture and placed it on the table between them.

"Your boys are quite young, here," he said.

"Myself and Charles, and that's Antoine on the right and Jean-Charles on the left."

"And about what age were your sons when this picture was taken?"

"Eleven and thirteen, I think." Henriette smiled as she gently drew her fingers across the surface of the glass. "It was a long-time ago."

"One more question, Madame. The nanny, what

happened to her?"

"She remained with us until she died. When Antoine was older and no longer needed her, she took on the day-to-day running of the household, and when the cook left, she took on all the catering for the family and all the events we held in the grounds. She died about five years after Antoine left."

"So your recipe has been passed on to your current cook?"

"I see what you are doing, Monsieur. By demonstrating to me that more than two people know of our dessert, you think I will drop my insistence that Antoine is still alive. I won't. Passing on a recipe is one thing but including personal family details in print is quite another. I know my son is alive."

***

Beth was in the back room of her new studio and shop carefully enclosing an old camera from the thirties in its brown leather case when Jacques arrived.

"Yet another sale from my on-line shop," she said after accepting a kiss. "And this is going to a collector in Brazil!" She reached across the worktop for a couple of sheets of tissue paper and began to wrap the case in it.

"I also have a little job for you, and you must invoice Vaux for this." Jacques retrieved the photo he had borrowed from Madame Beaufort. "I need both a digital copy and printed copies, please, so that I can return the original to my client."

Beth huffed and shrugged. "Oh, I'm not writing an invoice for that, Jacques. That's ludicrous. It'll take longer and cost more to process the payment than it will to do the job!"

"I will need at least six printed copies, Beth. That will be a genuine cost to your business, you know."

"That print is twenty by twenty-five, Jacques. Do you want the copies the same size?"

"No, something about half that size would be better."

Beth thought for a moment. "So a thirteen by eighteen copy would probably be best, and at 20 *centimes* each, that's an invoice for less than two Euros, Jacques. Just let me finish packaging this, and I'll do everything for you straight away." She lowered the wrapped camera and case into a small box and then packed scrunched up sheets of tissue paper around it. Closing the box, she sealed it and then applied an already prepared address label.

"All right," he said. "I give in, but whilst you are doing the work I will take your package to the Post Office. Deal?"

Beth smiled. "Yes." She handed him the box, and took the framed photo and placed it on the table facedown. Carefully pushing the stays back, she gently lifted out the backing. The back of the photo revealed a professional photographer's stamp and a date from 1976, but nothing else. She was a little surprised to find no handwritten notes stating who the people were. Removing it from the frame and placing it on the platen, she scanned an exact digital copy. Moving to the front of the shop, she took her place at the computer and navigated through to her software. She imported the new image and began to work on it.

Across one corner, the colours had faded where lengthy exposure to sunlight had gradually eaten away at the original brightness. A few slight tonal changes to that part of the photograph restored the evenness of colour across the whole picture. She zoomed in on the faces one by one and removed any slight imperfections. Returning the view to actual size, she made a slight adjustment to the contrast of the colours of the background. Satisfied, she saved her work, re-sized the photo, and printed the copies just as Jacques returned.

"Perfect timing," she said as she took the batch of copies from the printer tray and presented them to him. "And here's the original back in its frame, and, this afternoon, I'll set up an account for Vaux so that you can be invoiced monthly or quarterly for other work like this. OK?"

Jacques didn't respond. He just looked at the copies, then the original and the copies again. "The colours look slightly different," he said.

"They are, come round here and you can see exactly what I've done." Beth clicked back to the first image and zoomed in on the face of the smaller child on the right. "If you compare that with the framed original you'll see that everything is the same. When I move to the new image you'll see that the tiny blemish on his cheek here on the original has gone. I've coloured it out." Moving between the two pictures she showed Jacques the differences in the faces of the other three people. Zooming back out, she pointed out the slight tonal changes she had made to compensate for the fading from the sun.

"So, as far as other people are concerned, the copy is an exact replica apart from tiny blemishes and the background has been restored to its original colour. That's all."

Jacques studied the prints and the original. "Can you just go over that one more time, please, and zoom in on the faces again?"

Beth complied and, having made yet another comparison of the faces, Jacques eventually leaned back against the counter. "I don't think that boy is his son, is he?"

"Yes, I know," said Beth. "But he could be a cousin or maybe just a friend of the taller boy. You don't really know, and there's nothing on the back of the original to say who they are either."

"What was it about the photo that made you realise that the boy on the right may not be the man's son?"

"Same as you, I suppose. His eyes. The boy on the right has the same face shape and mouth as the woman, but he has blue eyes and blond hair. The taller boy on the left has brown eyes, the man's face-shape and nose and colouring. Both the adults have brown eyes. If they are the parents of one or both of the boys, then I thought brown-eyed parents couldn't have blue-eyed children. But ask one of your old contacts in pathology. They would know, wouldn't they?"

"Yes, they probably would. Thanks, Beth, and I'm heading back to the office. I'll be home late."

Before Beth had time to respond, Jacques was gone,

leaving the metal frame of the glass door of the shop to clang shut behind him. Beth scrunched her eyes shut, expecting the next sound to be the splintering of glass. But there was only the rattle of the door in the frame and the loud clunk of the latch. Clicking out of her software, she smiled to herself.

"Always a policeman, Jacques, and you always will be." She crossed the shop to the door, locked it and went into the other room. She still had two boxes of camera equipment that she had acquired from Old Thierry in Messandrierre to unpack, photograph for her on-line outlet, and to display in the shop.

***

"Didier, the original letter from Madame Beaufort, can I see it, please?" Jacques breezed through the almost deserted general office on the way to his own.

"It's on system, Jacques."

"The original paper copy, please." Jacques disappeared out of the door at the top of the room. Settled behind his desk, he took out his notebook and documented his latest theory, initialled and dated it.

"Here it is," said Didier, placing an open folder on the desk with the letter uppermost.

Jacques read through it and then examined it closely, flipping the paper over and back again. "What if Madame Beaufort hasn't been totally truthful with us, Didier?"

"In what way?"

"Look at this letter closely." Jacques turned the papers round to face his colleague and pointed to the most salient paragraph. "Look what she tells us. She lets us know that there has been a family argument, and she phrases it very elegantly. She ends with, 'It is my greatest wish that you find my son, Antoine'. But that is all she tells us about him. No date or place of birth. Nothing from which we can make a definite search. I had an idea earlier that maybe this letter was written some time ago, but it doesn't look like it."

"No, it looks recent to me. But, yes, I noticed the lack of detail about Antoine and told the admin staff to search backwards from last year. I thought I recognised the name and knew that, if I was right, we would find the record of the death and that could help us find the year of the birth. With that, I thought it would be clear if we had the right man."

"But she didn't send a photo either, did she?"

"No, the photos we have on file are from my ex-colleagues and, through them, from the passport office."

Jacques placed one of the prints that Beth had provided on the desk. "Take a look at that. A close look," he said. "What do you see?"

Didier picked up the print, shoved his spectacles up onto his forehead and peered at each member of the family in turn. "Those two boys may not be brothers, they are so different in colouring. I'm assuming this is the Beaufort family."

"Yes, it is. The boys in the photo are aged eleven and thirteen. But what if the eleven-year-old boy in that photo is not the boy who grew into the man in the photographs we have on file? The man that we think is Antoine Beaufort."

"How would we know that? Only Madame Beaufort can confirm that definitely or not. And she is convinced her son is still alive, isn't she?"

"Yes, but she has no direct evidence, Didier. So, what does she know that she's not telling us?"

Didier slumped down in the chair on the opposite side of the desk from Jacques. Arms across his chest, he stared at the wall above Jacques' head.

"Thinking about it, if that child in the photo, Antoine, is not Monsieur Beaufort's son, then whose is he? And, if Charles Beaufort found out he was not his son, it would provide a very solid explanation for the split in the family."

"A far better reason than the one we've already been given. This new possibility also raises some interesting questions, Didier. Who was Antoine's father? Where is he now? And why was the impact of the news on the family so devastating that Antoine felt he had to leave and never come back?"

"I agree. I also still want to know why he was there on the premises," added Didier. "Everything else we have suggests he had no reason to be in the restaurant at all on the night of the fire."

"Hmm. I wish I knew, and it's a question to which we need to find the right answer." Jacques drummed the fingers of his right hand on the desk. "Can we get these new photographs checked against the ones we already have to see what the similarities and differences are, please? And tomorrow, put two investigators on checking records and newspapers for everything there is about the Beaufort family. Madame must be in her eighties, her husband, Charles, is dead and would have been in his late eighties if he were still alive. So far, we haven't spoken to the older brother or any one of his children. My original thinking was that we wouldn't need to. Now, I'm not so sure. If there is some sort of a family secret, the brother will know something, even if he does not know all of the details."

"OK, leave that with me."

"Whilst you are dealing with that I want to press Pelletier for some more details on the fire, and I want to see Jonnie Berger again. I'm not convinced he has been totally honest with us either. The more I think about what he's told us, the more I think we should put a tail on him."

"I can set that up tomorrow if you wish?"

"No, let's wait until I get a response from Paris. I'm having the cookery schools checked to see if Chef Berger's information about Antoine's period of study there is true."

"Anything else, Jacques?"

"No, it's getting late. We'll pick all this up again tomorrow."

tuesday, june 14th

"...as you have seen, my team has been completely reshaped. In fact, only my role, that of Didier Duclos and his four colleagues on investigation, and two of the administrative roles have been retained from the original organisation." Jacques paused as the rest of the board members absorbed the new information.

Alain Vaux, at the head of the conference room table nodded, his face giving nothing away.

"Keeping the internal team small and discreet means that we can afford the external team of retained employees. Within this *département* we have on contract a number of people, all of whom have previously worked in the *gendarmerie* or the *police nationale,* who are available to us to call in for investigations as and when we need them. As a result, we can be more spontaneous and, at a lower cost, provide 24-hour surveillance as and when required. Region- and country-wide we have a second level of contract with a number of other security firms. Therefore, we can use their personnel for short periods, thereby reducing the need for us to send our own team members to other towns and cities and incur substantial travel and expenses costs."

Alain Vaux grinned at Mathieu Renaud, the Finance Director, who sat a couple places down to his right.

Jacques waited for a reaction but there was none. He continued with the final part of his presentation – the one that Beth had put together for him at the weekend.

"The last couple of slides examine the costs and the projected costs of my team for the coming year. Here, I have a month-by-month comparison of the last twelve months' costs measured against the same period in the

65

previous year. You can see that there has been a consistent fall in outgoings as I have gradually effected the changes within the team. At first, any money saved was small, but I believe the final figures speak for themselves."

"And finally, this last slide shows the projected costs for my team over the next twelve months, and there—"

"Just a moment," said Mathieu Renaud. A replacement for Roger Baudin, Mathieu had been headhunted by Alain Vaux from a rival company. A pinched expression permanently on his face, he had not endeared himself to his new colleagues since taking up his post.

"I hope these are not extrapolations, Monsieur Forêt. I have no interest in your capabilities with basic maths." Renaud stared at him over the top of his heavy-framed spectacles.

Jacques set his jaw before replying. "The actual figures for each of the budget heads are in the papers I handed out at the beginning of the meeting. This slide is a pictorial of that data."

Glancing at Alain, he continued. "My team will be making other savings for the group as a whole. With the restructuring and reduction in size of the internal team, the creation of the two-tier external team of investigators working from their own offices or homes, I am very confident that we can now relinquish the space we have been using on the third floor. As of Monday next week, that space will be available for other teams within the group to use or to rent out to other companies and so generate—"

"We will decide what income streams we need, Monsieur Forêt." Renaud cut in as he gestured to his colleagues around the table.

Alain Vaux nodded. "Thank you, Jacques." Turning his attention to Philippe Chauvin, he added, "IT Philippe, what have you to report?"

Back behind his own desk, Jacques was cradling a half-drunk cup of coffee in his hands as Alain walked in.

"Don't let Mathieu rattle you, Jacques," he said, closing

the office door behind him.

"I didn't think I did."

"You handled him well, and your presentation was detailed and well thought-out. But he got under your skin. I could see it in your eyes." Alain smiled and sat down. "I've known Mathieu a long time. He's very exacting, which is a good quality in an accountant in his position. But he can be very demanding, too, and sometimes deliberately obstructive if he thinks it will get him what he wants. He may manage the group finances, but it is myself and the board as a whole that make the decisions. You need to remember that." He paused. "May I give you a piece of advice?"

"Of course."

"Mathieu sees you as a policeman, not a manager. Only the other day, he mentioned to me that he thought the investigations arm of the business was a work area that we could do without. He believes that if we triple our payroll and pension payment contracts, we can generate a greater level of consistent and secure income for the group. Based purely on the numbers, I have to agree with him. He makes a convincing case. But I created this arm of the business, and I want to see it flourish under your leadership. But you need to take care, Jacques. Mathieu can be very persuasive and if he gets a few other members of the board thinking in the same way, I may not be able to save this part of the business. I realise that all the corporate-speak is difficult for you and that you are very used to working alone. But you are also part of the wider team at board level and you need to convince Mathieu of that. I've seen you lead investigations, Jacques. I know how single-minded and determined you are. You consistently get the best out of your people and, because of your success on other cases in the relatively short time you've been here, you have increased our work on investigations by 2.2%. But do I, or anyone else coming into this room, see that success?"

"I don't understand." Jacques thought for a moment and then shifted his gaze from Alain to his whiteboard and the different styles of writing, the different colours of marker used, determined by the person who had last updated it. Glancing around the room, he took in the piles of files on the small table on his left, the papers and notes on his desk. Thinking back to the clinical tidiness of the room when Alain used it, he felt a tightening in his gut. Everything suddenly seemed wrong, unprofessional.

I'm out of place.

"Think about it," said Alain. "How you handled Mathieu this morning was an excellent start. But you need to do more. You need to show him that, in the environment of the boardroom, you are just as single-minded and determined as you are when leading a case. OK?"

Jacques nodded and, in response, Alain swept out of his room.

"Damn it!" Jacques muttered under his breath. "And damn you, Renaud!" He slammed his coffee cup down on the desk, the dregs splashing out over his hand and onto the papers beneath.

In Pelletier's office, a few minutes walk away from his own, Jacques relaxed into a chair. The desk was covered with paper and files, the furniture was well worn, and the space exuded the care-worn sense of years of difficult criminal investigations. It felt comfortable and familiar. To Jacques it even smelt right. The desiccated mixture of ageing paper and dust softened with the faintest hint of the cleaner's once-a-month polish.

"Yes, I have it here," said Pelletier, a large file in front of him. "We did get a partial DNA match from the family. Madame Beaufort provided the sample for comparison herself. She also provided an old brush used by Antoine, from which we lifted some hair. With that, and the witness statements, the identity of the body was not really in doubt, Jacques."

Jacques let out a sigh. "OK, Bruno, but that's not what I was hoping to hear."

Pelletier shrugged. "Sorry, I can only tell you what we

have on file."

"Late yesterday, Didier and I were tossing a few ideas around. We can't seem to get to the real reason for Antoine being on the premises the night of the fire. The restaurant had been closed three days earlier with all the staff laid off. So why was he there, Bruno?"

"It was a question that concerned us at the time too. We interviewed all the employees as well as the chef and Vauclain. Only the chef and Vauclain were called to formally give evidence, and they both said they had not been aware that Beaufort was on the premises on the night of the fire."

"And when questioned about how he had access to the place after he had been laid off, what did they say?"

"They put forward different suggestions, but we couldn't find any substantiating evidence." Pelletier removed his spectacles and began to clean them.

"One theory that we came up with is that Beaufort had a set keys for the restaurant of his own, and you appear to be saying that that can't be true. Is that because there was no trace of his keys at the scene?"

"I'm saying we could not find any evidence to support any theory about why Beaufort was on the premises." Pelletier placed his polished glasses on the desk and pinched the bridge of his nose. "Whatever theory you want to come up with, Jacques, we have already thought of it. And I say, again, we couldn't find any substantiating evidence."

Jacques and Pelletier stared at each other as they weathered the strained silence.

"OK," said Jacques. "If everyone said they didn't know Beaufort was on the premises on the night of the fire, that leaves me with one supposition. He accessed the property using the same window at the back that the arsonist used."

Pelletier made no response. Jacques decided to move onto another matter. "The murder of Vauclain, do you think there is a connection between that and the fire in the restaurant in 2009. It's just that it seems odd that Vauclain should die shortly after I interviewed him for my enquiry."

Pelletier nodded his head. "We both know that I can't answer that question for you at this juncture. The murder enquiry has only just started. That, at least, is some confirmation for you. If I think there is a connection between Vauclain's death and your enquiry, I will let you know, and you will need to be formally interviewed, as I am sure you are aware. But, until then, there is nothing more I can say at the moment."

Jacques got up but as he was about to leave he posed one more question. "The missing knife, has that been found, and was it the murder weapon?"

"Yes, we have found the knife. I suspect it was the murder weapon, but forensics have it. I'm still waiting for their report."

Jacques was about to pose a supplementary question but stopped himself. Pelletier had a closed look on his face and he knew there was no more to be learned today. He left and made his way back to his office. As he walked across town, his phone signalled the arrival of a message. He ran across rue Théophile Roussel and pulled his phone out of his pocket once safely on the other side. The message was from his contact in Paris. He scrolled through the contents and then smiled to himself. *So, Monsieur Berger, I was right. You weren't telling the truth.*

At Hotel Claustres, Jacques was waiting for Dider to join him. Having asked the receptionist to let Chef Berger know that he'd arrived, Jacques made himself comfortable in a bucket chair in the foyer. He positioned it so that he could watch the comings and goings. Through the expanse of glass that fronted the building he spotted Didier on the opposite side of the street, waiting for a gap in the traffic. A few moments later, Jacques saw his colleague dodge around a white van, then sprint up the steps and into the foyer. Eventually, Didier settled into a chair opposite him and inclined his head in greeting.

Jacques maintained his observation. He'd noticed

something he didn't like.

"Dark-haired man, grey shirt, light jacket, dark trousers, over by reception going through the newspapers," Jacques said to Didier. "Now, he's moving over to the cluster of chairs on the far right. He followed you in. I'm sure he was the guy I saw in the red Renault Clio on the street outside the office the other day."

Didier nodded. "I'll get up and fetch a newspaper in a minute, and see if I recognise him." But before moving, Dider took his phone from his shirt pocket and scrolled through to the camera.

Jacques pulled out his notebook and pretended to check through the pages whilst he watched the dark-haired man. As expected, the suspect looked over the top of his newspaper as soon Didier got up.

"I'm certain you've got a tail," said Jacques when Dider returned to his seat. He glanced at his notebook. "And the registration number of the Renault he was using the other day is FN-229-RW. It's a local plate. If it's genuine, then we just need to know who he is and why he's following you. If not, then we need to be careful."

"I'll get it checked." Setting the paper aside, Didier texted one of his old colleagues.

"Monsieur Forêt, sorry to keep you waiting. What can I do for you?"

Jacques introduced Didier, and they both followed Jonnie Berger into a small private meeting room, furnished with a table and chairs for six, across the foyer.

"I've been checking the information you provided, Monsieur, and I have a few more questions as a result."

Berger nodded, but said nothing.

"You said that you paid most of the fees for Antoine Beaufort to attend a cookery school in Paris. I've had a contact of mine check the information you provided and we've traced the school. We have confirmed that Antoine did attend and was enrolled on a short, intensive course but his fees were paid for in part by a Jean-Luc Sault, with the balance paid for by Jean-Charles Beaufort, Antoine's older brother." Jacques looked up from his notes expecting a reply.

The chef remained silent.

"Nothing to say, Monsieur?"

Berger shrugged and smiled. "I had no idea his brother had paid part of the cost. As far as I knew he hadn't been in contact with his family since he left home."

"I'm more interested in your explanation of why you told us you had paid most of the fees when in fact they were paid by someone with a completely different name."

Jacques watched closely as the chef appeared to have a mental debate with himself.

"It's a very straight forward question, Monsieur. Did you pay for Antoine Beaufort's fees or not? And if you did, why does the payment appear in someone else's name?"

"Administrative error on the part of the school?" Berger pushed back his cuff to check his watch.

"Look, Monsieur, you can save us all a lot of time and tell us exactly what happened, or we can undertake the necessary checks to find this Jean-Luc Sault. We already know from the school that his contact address was in Le Puy at the time of the payment. Didn't you say you were working in Le Puy when you paid Antoine Beaufort's fees?"

Berger looked around the room, the thumb and forefinger of his right hand constantly twisting one of the buttons on his chef's jacket.

"All right," he said eventually. "All right! But it's not what you might think. Jean-Luc Sault is my real name. I changed it to Jonnie Berger because of the books. My agent suggested that I come up with something a little less traditionally French than my real name. We agreed on Jonnie Berger because the pronunciation is immediately obvious and it works well in the US, Canada and other English-speaking areas of the world, which is where I get most of my book sales."

"And is it still just the name you use as an author?"

"No, I've legally changed my name to Jonnie Berger now. I can show you the documents if necessary."

Jacques shook his head. "Just one more small point. 7000 euros is a lot of money to pay out for a casual acquaintance, Monsieur Berger."

The look of anger in Berger's eyes was not lost on Jacques. But the speed with which his interviewee brought his evident distaste for the implication raised by his question under control impressed him.

"As I've said before, Monsieur Forêt, I was giving back. I was allowing a great friend to take an opportunity that would have been denied him otherwise."

"It's still a lot of money as a…gift, shall we call it?"

Berger's eyes narrowed and he took a deliberate breath. "I've given you my answer. I have nothing more to say." Glancing at his watch again, he stood. "I have work to do," he said. "If you need anything else, you know how to find me." He marched out of the room.

Didier's wry look echoed Jacques' own thoughts. "Yes, he's very practised at handling us, isn't he? He's going to be difficult to crack."

"What do you want to do?"

"Close the door, and we'll take advantage of the isolation to work out our next steps."

Jacques flicked through his notes. "I want a full trace on Jean-Luc Sault," he said once Didier was back at the table. "I want to know everything from the moment he was born."

"OK, I'll make a start on that. What about putting a tail on him?"

Jacques thought for a moment. "We've got our own tail that we need to deal with first."

"I managed to get a photo of his reflection in the mirrors behind reception when I went to get the newspaper. I've seen him before. I'll get a search done and see what we can find."

Jacques nodded. "You go now and make sure you leave the door wide open. I'll observe and then leave in about ten minutes, and we'll meet back at the office tomorrow morning." Jacques moved to the other side of the table where he had an almost complete view of the hotel foyer through the open door.

Didier walked out and strode across to the main entrance. Jacques, head positioned as though scrolling through his messages on the phone in his hand, watched as the man with the newspaper glanced first in his direction and then over to Didier.

A moment later, the stranger had discarded the newspaper and was on his feet. As he reached the entrance and stepped out into the bright afternoon sunshine, he took out his phone and made a call. Strolling down the front steps, he turned to take the same direction as Didier.

Jacques put his notebook away. *That call was for backup, I think.* He strode over to reception.

"I'm running late for my next appointment and I need to be on the street that runs behind the hotel. Is there another way out?"

"Yes, Monsieur. Take the lift to the basement car park and follow the exit signs."

Jacques nodded his thanks, checked the foyer once more, and then disappeared into the lift alone.

***

Think I've been spotted. My mark has been leading me all over the city.

17.12

Leave it. Pick this up tomorrow.

17.13

wednesday, june 15th

"The registration that I had checked yesterday belongs to a Toyota Rav4 that was reported stolen two weeks ago." Didier slid a photo of the vehicle across the desk to Jacques. "I would expect that the Renault now bearing those plates is also stolen."

"I agree, and there's probably a third man with another car that we haven't spotted yet, also stolen and with false plates. With two of us to follow, there have to be at least three people undertaking the surveillance. But why? And if it is connected with either Beaufort or Vauclain, how did they know we are involved?"

"I can get a couple of contacts from outside the *département* to help us spring a trap for our tails, and then we can confront them."

Jacques pushed his chair away from his desk. "I'd rather wait until we had more detail on the case. If we set up something like that, I want to know what I'm dealing with. Can you get the work to uncover Jonnie Berger's background completed as a priority, please? There might be something there that will help us."

"I've already got one of the admin team at the library going through newspapers and his books for hints about his background. I've also got an investigator working on online searches for anything he can find. And, whilst you are out this afternoon, I will be working through archival records and talking to his colleagues."

"What about the information we got from Vauclain's place on Monday, and all the telephone numbers that needed to be checked?"

"Not much to go on. The number on the back of the

postcard was a pay-as-you-go phone and is no longer active. The other numbers in his phone have all been checked and the owners of all of them, apart from one, are genuine and belong to people who actually knew Vauclain on a personal level. The last one, number ending 4591 is another pay-as-you-go that appears to be still active but as yet I haven't been able to get a response to my calls or texts."

Jacques nodded his approval. "Something that has just occurred to me, Didier. Apart from our own team, who else might know that we are looking for Antoine Beaufort?"

"Well, almost anyone in the *département* could know. When the original letter came in, the admin team took the usual steps, including placing a discreet notice asking for information in the personal column of the local paper."

"And the response?"

"Nothing especially helpful, so far. But I can let you have the latest version of the report if you wish."

Jacques nodded. "And one last thing, Didier. Is there an e-version of the local paper available?"

Didier shrugged. "I'm not sure, Jacques. I collect my copy from the *Tabac* on rue Soubeyran on the way into work. But if there is an e-copy, then almost anyone, anywhere, might know that we are looking for Beaufort."

"OK, and thanks." Jacques scowled and, hands in his trouser pockets, he strolled over to the windows and looked at the street below. Rather than just let his mind wander as he vaguely watched people and cars as they passed, this time he carefully and systematically scanned the view from one edge of his vision to the other. He mentally noted the positions of the parked cars, their colour and make, as best as he could guess without being able to make-out the manufacturer's decal. He scrutinised the people and made particular note of the man sitting at a pavement *café* opposite. *So, you are here again.* Picking up his phone, he ran out of the office and down the stairs to the ground floor. Only one man was at the security desk in reception. Jacques slipped into the second seat.

"The cameras on the exterior of the building, which are

they?"

"You need to be on view for camera 1 or 2, Monsieur Forêt," the security guard said as he reached across and tapped the keyboard.

Jacques scanned the monitor. "And if I want to have the view on full screen rather than split?"

The guard tapped another key. The screen changed and Jacques peered at it. "That man there," he said. "How long has he been there?"

"He was there when I came on shift an hour ago. I can check the tapes for earlier."

"Yes, please, and let Didier Duclos know what you've found." Jacques glanced at his watch. "I'm out for the rest of the day, so if Didier needs any more footage from the tapes, please deal with it immediately."

The guard nodded and Jacques sprinted back to his office to collect his jacket, bag, and a small gift for Beth that he'd bought a couple of weeks earlier.

***

With the banners mounted on their individual supporting frames, Beth was able to fix them to the floor and ceiling fittings to the right of the shop window. She chose the one for autumn as the backdrop for her display for the formal opening of the shop. Carefully rolling the remaining banners, she picked them up and carried them into the back room.

Following the fire in October 2009, the property had been substantially improved. As she walked through the connecting door, she breathed in the still just discernible smell of newness. The window at the back had been replaced and fitted with a new electronic metal shutter, the interior had been re-plastered and painted white, and a large sail had been erected to provide a clean white ceiling and cover for the dark wood of the old beams that had required repair, significant refurbishment, and re-staining. On the wall opposite the window were a set of newly fitted drawers and cupboards to store her cameras, equipment and now, specially-created storage for the banners. She slid out the wide drawer and slotted them in. Turning around, she surveyed the room and grinned with pleasure at the sight of it.

In the shop area, she began to unpack the boxes of sale items that had been delivered that morning and arranged them on the invisible shelving that she had insisted was fitted. The property owner had suggested a much cheaper range of fitments, but Beth had been intransigent. Having waited more than a year for the property to be repaired following the fire, she had felt she almost had a right to demand what she wanted inside. But that hadn't stopped the owner from notifying her of a rent increase at the earliest legal opportunity.

Collapsing the box she had just emptied, Beth looked up to see Jacques standing at the door, arms full with a large heavy package, smiling at her.

"Well, you're a welcome change from the usual sort of delivery man I have been getting around here." She grinned as she held the door open.

"These books are heavy, and there's another two boxes," he said, hefting the parcel onto the counter. As Beth toed a wedge into place under the door, Jacques breezed past her to fetch another container from the boot of her car.

Using the silver letter opener that had been her grandmother's, Beth sliced through the tape on the first box. She pulled the flaps open, carefully removed the scrunched up brown packing paper, and lifted out one of the books. Some specks of paper dust clung to the shiny new dust jacket. She blew them away and ran her hand over the photograph that comprised the panoramic view stretching across the front and back covers.

"That's the last one." Jacques placed the third box on the floor next to the second. Straightening, he massaged his back. "I've got the champagne for tomorrow in the boot as well. Do you want me to bring that in?"

"Yes, please. It can go in the fridge in the small kitchen

upstairs."

Jacques darted out again and returned with the box of wine, his jacket lying on top.

"So this is the latest collection of Old Thierry's photographs," he said as he slid the carton on to the end of the counter.

"Yes, and sort of, no." Beth removed the dust jacket and laid it out in front of her. "The dust jacket is a new addition and the photo, which took me two days to get right, is a current version of one of Old Thierry's photos in the book. The text has been expanded, and I've added in some more of Thierry's shots."

Jacques picked up a copy of the book and began leafing through it as he edged in front of Beth. "Don't look up from the book, Beth, and just listen to what I'm going to say."

Beth caught her breath and nodded but wondered what was coming next.

"There's a man in the *pâtisserie* across the road who followed me here from the office. I need to shake him off. I'm going to take the wine and the other boxes through to the back, and then I'll duck out of the window in there. After about ten minutes, move the car round to the back. OK?"

Beth, still turning the pages of the book, looked up at him. "Got that," she said, a tremor in her voice.

"There's nothing for you to worry about. It's me he's interested in, not you."

"OK." She forced a weak smile across her face.

"I'm going to move and as soon as I do, start talking to me about the book as though we're having a normal conversation."

"I don't know what to say."

"Anything. He can't hear you. He just needs to think that I'm still here. Tell me anything."

"OK." She glanced at the open page in the book in her hands. "This is one of Thierry's oldest photographs. I thought I should include it just because of its age rather than the quality of the shot. In reality, it's not that good a picture." She followed Jacques through to the back room as he moved first one box and then the other. "Unfortunately, the building in the background doesn't exist anymore, so I couldn't get a more up to date version and—"

"This time just follow me to the doorway, then stay there and keep talking." Jacques lifted the box of wine and disappeared into the second room.

Beth positioned herself at the doorway and leaned against the jamb, book still in her hands and her voice tremulous as she continued to talk. When she heard Jacques click the window shut she moved into the back room and collapsed against the worktop to get her breath. She checked her watch. *About another five or six minutes to go.*

"I can do this," she told herself. "I can do this. I just need to keep talking and stay calm." Shoulders back, she stood straight, fixed a smile on her face and walked back into the shop.

"I'm going to put some of the books on the medium display block that I bought a couple of months ago and an open copy of the book on the easel in the window, and that should give me an opportunity to check that the man is still there. And he is. Good. OK, so now I should be able to go and get the car keys and move the car."

Certain that Jacques had had enough time to disappear, she collected her bag, locked the window at the back and paused for a few moments to take some deep breaths. Her energy replenished and her back ramrod straight, she marched through to the shop, out of the front door, locking it behind her, and got in the car without looking at the man in the *pâtisserie*. As she drove off, she saw him come out onto the street in her rear view mirror. He didn't look pleased. She didn't care. She was in the car and away from him, and Jacques was somewhere else in town and safe and that was all that mattered.

***

In Messandrierre, Delacroix's plans for his first few days of the new week had not worked out as he'd hoped. His trip to Mende on Monday had been useful. He'd found a small shop in the old Jewish quarter that sold militaria, stamps and coins, and other bits of mostly worthless bric-a-brac. The owner, an elderly gentleman a little unsteady on his feet, but with a mind as sharp as a razor, had been only too happy to help.

Accepting the printed list of the coins that Delacroix had prepared, he had taken his time running through the first few pages. Delacroix had waited patiently until the man had said that he would be happy to complete a full valuation. He went on to point out that, without seeing the precise condition of the coins, any valuation he would be making would have to be regarded as an estimate. Delacroix smiled to himself as he recalled recognising how astute and careful the old man had been. He always respected people who took the same approach to business as he did.

Unfortunately, the delay in the coin shop meant that the florist had to take an order for flowers, as they didn't have either the time or the full stock for the arrangement that he had wanted. So, here he was at the farmhouse, pacing the floor in his refurbished attic with its panoramic windows on one side, waiting for his delivery. And Delacroix hated to be kept waiting. If anyone was going to be kept waiting it was other people, his business associates or whoever, just not him.

From his vantage point, he saw the florist's van turn into the village about twenty minutes later than anticipated. Having dressed appropriately – black tie, white shirt, black business suit – he wanted to make sure he got every possible advantage, in the eyes of the villagers, from the visit to the family grave. He moved down the stairs swiftly and out onto the front porch – another improvement he had made to the property.

Standing tall and sombre on his recently laid, but short drive, he let the florist pull up in front him and graciously accepted the floral display. Pausing for a few moments, to ensure that the 'stage' was entirely his own, he looked over the village. *Fermier* Rouselle was on his way back to his property in his tractor. Madame Pamier was making her way to the cemetery as she did regularly. *Maire* Mancelle was on the main street talking to *Père* Chastain. Couldn't be better, Delacroix thought. He took his first steps along his drive and then out onto the top road. He followed it along until it intersected with the main street that ran through the village.

As he passed his neighbours he made a point of greeting them respectfully. At the tall ironwork cross that marked the entrance to the village, he paused for a moment, as if remembering the prayer that was uttered there for his uncle on the day of the funeral. At least, that was what he was hoping his current audience of villagers would think and repeat to others.

The cattle tunnel had been closed and filled in as had been promised by the *préfecture*. He had no idea exactly when the work had been completed, but he had heard enough to know that it had caused a small revolution amongst the inhabitants of Messandrierre. On he strode across the RN88 and then along the rough path on the other side up to the cemetery. At the entrance, he realised that he wasn't entirely sure that he could remember exactly which grave and memorial belonged to the Delacroix family. He made a point of taking a full tour of all the graves. It was a very small village and the number of family graves was equally small.

Madame Pamier was on her knees, arranging flowers.

"A sad duty, Madame," he said in his Canadian French as he paused by her family grave. "But necessary. It's important to remember our lost loved ones."

Madame Pamier gave him the briefest of looks, a barely perceptible nod in response and continued with her work.

Having spotted his uncle's grave in the next row, Delacroix moved on. Standing in front of the grey granite monument he waited, head bowed in respect. As soon as he heard Madame Pamier's footsteps on the gravel path, he turned to see where she was. He smiled to himself as he watched her small figure disappear through the gate. Confident that the high stone walls of the cemetery would cover his next actions, he retrieved his phone. Squatting down, he angled the device so that he could capture all the names and dates of birth and death of the various generations of the Delacroix family interred there. He took half a dozen shots to be sure. His real business done, he stood and assumed his sombre alter ego. Eventually, he placed the flowers at the front of the monument and stood in what he hoped would be construed as quiet contemplation by anyone else who might be passing or visiting.

As he turned to leave, *Père* Chastain entered. Delacroix nodded a greeting to him and made his way slowly through the graves to the entrance. He continued his slow and reverent progress through the village until he reached the farmhouse. Once his front door was closed behind him he pulled off his tie and jacket, went straight to his *cave* and got himself a beer. The afternoon sun had been just a little too hot for this particular ruse.

***

From the dark shadows of an alley at the back of Hôtel Claustres, Jacques observed every vehicle that came and went from the underground car park that afternoon. At a little after four, his patience was rewarded. A silver BMW emerged with Jonnie Berger at the wheel. Jacques quickly captured a photo on his phone and made a mental note of the registration. Moving to the other side of the alley, he tapped his contacts list and called one of his associates who was parked nearby and waiting for instructions.

"Silver BMW, registration BE-237-AB, he's just turned right into avenue Foch, heading west."

Jacques walked the few metres to the junction of the alleyway with avenue Foch. He turned left and headed towards the internal ring road and Beth's shop. Although his tail was gone, Jacques was still wary. He sprinted across the main road, dodging the traffic and, once in the cover of a narrow side street, stopped and checked to see if anyone was following. The street was empty, but still he didn't move for at least ten minutes. Then he continued a little further and ducked into a ginnel and waited. The only passer-by was a woman with a pram who entered a property on the other side of the alleyway. Back in the sunshine and content that he really was alone, Jacques casually strode through the old heart of Mende to where Beth's car was parked at the back of the shop.

thursday, june 16th

Jacques gathered his papers from the dining table and packed them into his bag. Taking a last slurp of coffee as he moved across to the kitchen, he dumped his cup on the draining board.

"Beth, I'm going," he shouted as he slipped his arms into his jacket. He patted his pocket and pulled out the small gift he had kept in his desk drawer for over two weeks and placed it in the centre of the table. The pale blue bow looked a little crumpled. He straightened it as best he could.

"Coming," she shouted from the bedroom at the other side of the apartment. A few seconds later, Beth ran into the living space, her shoulder-length hair neatly combed, her dress not quite properly fastened at the back, attempting to put her shoes on and walk at the same time.

"Zip me up, will you?" She spun around, one shoe on, the other in her left hand.

"There's no need to rush. I'm walking to the office this morning," he said, gently planting a kiss on her neck. "You've planned thoroughly for today, and everything will go well. I know it."

"I hope so. And you'll be there at three?"

"I wouldn't miss it." Collecting his bag he moved to the door. "I've got to go – and there's a surprise for you on the table," he said as he disappeared into the vestibule. Not quite closing the door completely, he waited. The muffled shriek of delight as Beth opened her gift was the only reward he required. Quietly letting himself out of the front door, he ran down the four flights of stairs, a contented smile on his face.

At just after ten, Jacques walked into the general office to begin his regular 'catch-up' meeting. Didier was handing out various reports and documents to all those present. Jacques had his own set of papers which he'd scrutinised since arriving that morning. Taking his seat at the side of Didier's desk, he was presented with a cup of coffee by Amélie, a member of the admin team. Pregnant with her first child and married to Maxim, her counter-part on admin, she had been with the Vaux organisation for about eight years and had an extensive working knowledge of personnel policies. Her husband had joined the group within a few months of Amélie, and their blossoming romance had been the talk of the office ever since, until they eventually married in April 2010.

Amélie opened the meeting as she always did with a brief summary of spending within the team.

"I have just one comment," said Jacques as he cast his eye across the spreadsheet. "Can we keep a close watch on expenses, please? We have some new people working for us on retained contracts, and we need to be sure they adhere to our strict rules when making claims."

"They've all been taken through our procedures by myself and Maxim, and they know that their claims are under a 100% check for the first month of their work with us. It has also been made clear to them that we consider a month to be twenty-eight cumulative days of work for us rather than a straight calendar month."

"Thanks, Amélie. That's good to know." Jacques moved through his sheaf of papers to the next report. He flicked through a couple of the pages and then placed the lot on Didier's desk. "I'll take everything in my own order of importance, I think. Jonnie Berger. First, his own personal history. Where are we with that?"

"Maxim has been following that through," said Didier as he nodded to his colleague to take the floor.

"You'll see from the notes that I've got confirmed dates of birth along with details of parents and siblings. Berger was born on a farm at the edge of a small village in the *département* of Alpes-de-Haute-Provence. He was educated locally, but his mother died when he was only six years old. Berger and his younger sister and brother were then brought up in care. The father and his two eldest sons remained on the farm. I'm still checking specifics of his work history and his business dealings."

"And the tail we put on him yesterday afternoon and evening, what did we get out of that?"

"That did throw up something quite interesting. He has another property in Les Alpiers. It's a small mountain village about forty kilometres east of here."

"Yesterday, when I saw him leave the hotel he was heading west out of the city," said Jacques. "Where did he go?"

"He went to see a supplier in Marvejols and arrived at Les Alpiers at around 21.30."

Jacques thought for a moment and grimaced. "So he wasn't at the hotel for the evening shift. Interesting. On the bike it takes me about twenty minutes to do the journey from here to Marvejols and from there to Les Alpiers... I could do that in about forty-five, maybe fifty minutes. So that leaves around four hours. That's a long time to spend with one supplier."

"The supplier is a Madame Sylvie Giroux of *Épicerie Giroux et Fils*. The business is in the husband's name, but it was Madame Giroux that Chef Berger met."

"And four hours is still a long time to spend talking about herbs, spices and groceries." Jacques grinned. "Perhaps we have found his Achilles' heel."

Didier let out a snort of laughter and Maxim glanced at his wife before continuing. "There's something else which I wasn't able to check until I arrived this morning. The property that Chef Berger went to in Les Alpiers, according to the voters' list, is inhabited by a Monsieur G A Sault, that's his younger brother, and a Monsieur J-L Sault."

"And Jean-Luc Sault is Jonnie Berger's name by birth," said Jacques. "He has a suite of rooms at the hotel. I thought they were his registered address for voting purposes and all relevant municipal and civic obligations."

"They are and I've cross-checked that. What I don't understand is how it is possible for him to have two sets of voting papers. To vote, he has to be registered with the *préfecture*, and they would have noticed, wouldn't they? It's election fraud, isn't it?" Maxim addressed his question directly to Jacques.

"Not necessarily. People move address and mostly just register at their new location. Chef Berger has been working outside of this *département* for a considerable number of years. I can see how a possible duplicate registration could occur as a result. But fraud, we would have to prove intent and that is not our purpose, Maxim. But thank you for bringing this to my attention and when this case is concluded, if we believe there was intent, then we will have to prepare a report detailing our evidence and pass it on."

Maxim accepted the proposal with a reluctant nod. "The other thing that I have checked out is whether Monsieur Giroux is still around. He is registered, along with his wife, as a voter at the address of the shop. He and his wife live above the business premises. Maurice, their son, lives in Marvejols also, but on the other side of town."

"Do we have any information on whether Monsieur Giroux was at home yesterday evening?"

Maxim grinned. "Monsieur Giroux was not seen by our man yesterday at all, so I telephoned the shop this morning and asked to speak to him. Madame Giroux answered and told me that he was away on business and would not be back until tomorrow afternoon. I let her think I would call back and left it at that."

"Well done! We'll make an investigator of you yet, Maxim." A wide and knowing grin spread across Jacques' face. "I suppose we can all imagine how the afternoon and early evening went for Berger and Madame! OK, next the accidental hunting incidents that we seem to have had on our case list for far too long – why are we making no progress?"

"We followed the agreed additional lines of questioning,"

said Didier, "but have come up with nothing. The police are still maintaining there is not enough, nor any new, evidence for them to re-open the cases and the bullets extracted from the bodies have not been matched to any other incidents or known or recovered weapons."

Jacques frowned. "Two more victims like Juan de Silva and no resolution for the families except an inexplicable loss." He let out a deep sigh. "All right. We close these cases and stop working on them, but we keep them on file."

"I'll calculate the costs for our services and move the files to the amber list," said Maxim. "Will you want to see the invoices before I send them?"

"I'll leave it to your discretion, Maxim. But I don't want the respective families charged unnecessarily for our services as we still haven't got a clear answer for them."

Maxim nodded and jotted a note.

"The matrimonial cases: I see two of those are now resolved."

"Yes, both are seeking legal advice, which I expect will end in divorce proceedings," said Didier. "The invoices will be out by Friday. The third case is not progressing well. We're using one of our newly contracted retainees, as the location is St-Étienne. He keeps on turning in his expenses but still no new evidence and no real conclusion."

"It shouldn't take more than two to four weeks to resolve this sort of case."

"I agree. Do you want me to go up there and see what's really happening?"

"No, I need you here, Didier. Maxim, can you find out what's going on with this case, please, and if necessary, go up there yourself and talk to the investigator."

Maxim nodded, jotted a line on a note and stuck it to his monitor.

"So, we come to the Beaufort case and our friends who insist on following us everywhere. Didier?"

"The tails we've collected are from Marseille. Your tail is Marc Meyer and the other is Jean Allard. Both known to the police and with numerous convictions for assault, aggravated assault and other similar offences. In addition, they have both been under investigation several times before for numerous other offences of a similar nature but, because of lack of evidence, no formal charges have been brought or the cases have been dropped."

"We need to watch our step. Do we know who they are working for?"

Didier shook his head. "They each have their own turf in and around Marseille, and they both have connections to the Devereux brothers. I've asked my old snouts to keep their eyes open and to ask around to see if they can find anything for us."

"And the research into the Beaufort family?"

"Madame Henriette Claudine Beaufort, previously de Garmeaux, was born in Passy—"

"Passy! Are you sure about that?" Jacques interrupted. "You do mean Passy in Paris, don't you?"

Didier nodded and checked his notes. "Yes, Passy, Paris in 1925. She was the eldest of three sisters. Henriette and her sisters are first generation Parisians, but the de Garmeaux family originally came from the *département* of Manche in the north. Madame's mother was from Côtes-d'Armor, on the northern coast of the *Bretagne* peninsula, and her maiden name was Le Bresco. The Le Bresco family also has land and assets mostly in Côtes-d'Armor and the neighbouring *département* of Finistère."

"1925, so that would make Henriette—"

Didier supplied the answer before Jacques could complete the mental mathematics. "Eighty-six. Her birthday was two days ago on the 14th. She was educated in Paris at the same exclusive girls' school as her two younger sisters. Next, she appears in an article in a gossip magazine. She's in a photograph with two other women at a very posh birthday party at the age of twenty-five. Interestingly, if you look carefully at the photo, you'll see that the man standing behind her is Charles Beaufort." Didier slid the copy of the article across to Jacques.

"Where's this?"

"In Le Puy."

"So, she was here in this area even earlier than we first thought. This would be 1950."

Didier nodded and then continued, "She married Charles Beaufort in April 1963, at the age of 37 and their eldest son, Jean-Charles Michel Beaufort, was born seven months later in November 1963 and Antoine Charles Maximilian Beaufort was born around eighteen months later in April 1965."

"That's interesting. Was Jean-Charles a full-term baby, do we know?"

Didier consulted his notes. "We have a copy of an announcement in the newspaper which states that Jean-Charles was a 'healthy boy weighing 3.6 kilos'. Both my sons were full term and both weighed around 3 kilos, so, yes I'd say that was full-term."

Jacques nodded. "Her marriage may have been for necessity. It's also interesting that Madame Beaufort was thirty-seven years old when she married. A bit surprising, considering her family connections in Paris. Passy is the 16th *arrondissement*, Didier. You need to own a bank to be able to afford to live there. Property in that part of Paris is much sought after and very expensive. Her family must have been very wealthy. Do we know the exact place she was born and how they acquired their wealth?"

Didier checked his notes. "She was born in an apartment in Place Alboni."

Jacques' eyes widened. "Apartments there cost millions today," he said. A frown gathered on his forehead as he asked himself why someone from such a prosperous family, with all that Paris had to offer, had apparently spent her adult life in the solitude and quiet of the Cévennes. An echo moved across his mind as he thought back to his interview with her. What was it she'd said? Jacques rose and went over to the windows. *Something about mental strength.* As he gazed down on the street below he posed the question, why? He thought back to the day of his visit and the care-worn state of Henriette's room. *There's something not right here.*

Jacques turned. "Sorry, Didier. Continue please." Focused and listening intently, he resumed his place.

"The de Garmeaux family has extensive tracts of land in the north, residential property in Paris and Lyon, but their most significant wealth came originally from arms and armaments during the first world war. They moved to the apartment in place Alboni in 1921. The apartment is now occupied by Henriette Beaufort's youngest sister, her eldest son and his wife and the youngest of their four children who is at university in Paris. The middle sister died in 1944."

Jacques frowned. "We're missing something here. Henriette is the oldest of three daughters. Why has the family home, a very valuable piece of property, apparently only been inherited by the youngest daughter and her offspring? Was Henriette's share bought out? If so, do we know what happened to the money? It would have been a significant payout."

"Yes, I see what you mean. It's not that simple, Jacques. The property was purchased by the company when Henriette's grandfather was still principal owner. It remains a company asset. The youngest daughter married her grandfather's company secretary who was gifted, on marriage, a sizable portion of shares in the company. Henriette's father and his then son-in-law took over the company once the old man became to ill to manage it. The company remains in the families' hands even now as de Garmeaux Associates. What's of particular interest is that at no time has Henriette or her husband been listed as any part of DGA."

"A daughter estranged, perhaps. And if so what would be the reason?" Jacques began pacing the room again, hands in his trouser pockets and eyes firmly fixed on his shoes as he moved. And a second echo passed through his conscious thoughts. '*I've always been mentally strong. I've always had to be.*' Again he asked himself, why?

He wandered back to his seat. "I wonder if some aspects of this case relate to an earlier period of Madame Beaufort's life. Have we checked what happened to her prior to her marriage?"

Didier shook his head. "Only as far back as 1950. We seem to lose track of her before that until we reach the school records. But we can pick that up and follow it through tomorrow."

"Good work, and can we get that missing information as soon as possible, please? Next, the bank statements we found at Vauclain's, I've been through those and there's something I don't understand. Where's the money?"

Didier frowned. "What do you mean?"

"The money from the insurance payout. It must have been substantial. So, where is it?"

Didier shrugged. "It would have been paid out almost a year ago. It could have been used for any number of things by now… Invested in stocks or shares or some sort of insurance or pension plan. It could be invested in a new business—"

"Exactly!" Jacques drummed his fingers on Didier's desk. "Vauclain was a business man. His last known business premises were destroyed by fire in 2009. He was murdered a few days ago, and it appears that, between 2009 and his death, there has been no new business venture. So what happened to the money?"

Didier frowned. "Are you sure you want to pursue that? Vauclain is dead. His death may be connected with our current enquiry in relation to Beaufort, but we cannot be sure about that at the moment. Shouldn't we be looking for connections between Beaufort and Vauclain instead?"

"Yes, you're right. We need to find out as much as we can about the people that both Vauclain and Beaufort associated with. That payout could have been used for anything, including a pay-off. The money could be the link between Vauclain and Beaufort. Follow the money, Didier."

He stood and moved towards his own office but halted at the door. "Something else has just occurred to me. That place of Vauclain's was spotless. I'm betting he won't have done the housework himself. See if you can find out if he had a cleaner. Check the local domestic cleaning companies here in Mende and get someone out to Montbel to make discreet enquiries. It's quite likely it was a local woman who lived in the village. And don't forget to check the *petites annonces* on the board in the supermarket there. If his cleaner is local, that is where we will find her because she will probably need to replace the income she has now lost."

The formal opening of Beth's shop was going well. From his allotted station behind the counter, Jacques could almost join every conversation. His initial task was to hand out the welcome glasses of champagne or juice as everyone arrived. That job completed, he decided to take a glass for himself. Catching the eyes of *Fermier* Rouselle and his wife, who were chatting to Gaston and Marianne over by the banner in the front window, he raised his flute to them. The owner of the *pâtisserie* across the road was in deep conversation with Marie and Martin Mancelle to the right of the window. In the back room he could hear Beth chatting to Monsieur Rochefort – the local printer – Madame Pamier and *Maire* Mancelle. On his left, Pierre was flicking through the display of large mounted photographs one after the other. Jacques let the various conversations slip out of his conscious mind and observed the boy for a moment.

"Something on your mind, Pierre?"

"No." Keeping his back to Jacques, he began flipping the pictures in the opposite direction.

"A little bored, perhaps? Or just not happy with your photograph on the banner?"

"No, I like it," he said, carefully positioning the display so that only the first photograph could be seen. "I don't look like that anymore, so no-one will really know it's me." He turned. "I'm thinking about something important." A serious look on his face, he shoved his hands in the pockets of his shorts and sauntered over to Jacques. "It's nothing," he said as he lounged against the wall behind the counter.

"If it's important, it can't be nothing. Do you want to tell me about it?" Jacques wondered if there was a problem at school. Pierre had recently moved to the school in Badaroux because he hadn't settled at the one in Châteauneuf, and Marie had had some concerns about his teacher there.

Pierre frowned. "What's it like to have a sister?"

Taken aback, Jacques drained the last of his wine and carefully placed the empty glass on the counter. He wondered how he had failed to notice that Marie was pregnant and quickly stole a look at her. He could see no discernible change and decided that must be because it was too early for it to be obvious.

"A sister? Well, that's wonderful news, Pierre." A thought occurred to him. "Are you sure your *maman* is happy for me to know about this?"

"I think so. *Maman* and *papa* have been talking about it for months, and now it's really going to happen."

"All right, well, having a sister is a wonderful thing. But when she first arrives you will need to look after her very carefully."

"Yes, I know. *Maman* explained. She will be going to my old school at first and then she'll be coming to my new one. She's called Célestine and she's six years old."

Jacques' momentary confusion cleared. "Ah, I see. As her older brother it will be up to you to make sure she settles in at school."

Pierre nodded as a clouded frown spread across his face. "But will she want to help with my police work?"

Jacques grinned. *So that's the real problem.* "She might want to join the police herself when she's older. You should ask her. Would it be so bad if she did want to help with your investigations?"

Pierre thought for a moment. "*Gendarme* Clergue says police work needs a clear head and a sharp mind, and *papa* says that girls are very emotional. I'm not sure she would be any good at police work."

Jacques chewed the inside of his cheek to stave off his need to laugh at the naivety of the boy's path of logical thought.

"I think you should give her a chance, Pierre. She might surprise you. My sister Thérèse is a couple of years older than me, but we have always looked out for each other. One thing I do know about sisters is that they give you very good and honest advice. Sometimes, they can be brutally honest, but that's usually because you need them to be, even if you don't realise it yourself. They are also very useful for getting you introductions to the prettiest girls in school."

"Girls! I haven't got time for girls." Pierre huffed, helped himself to a glass of juice and disappeared into the back room.

"You will have soon enough," Jacques murmured to himself.

***

In the back room, Beth smiled as Pierre presented himself at the side of the *Maire*, glass in his right hand and his left draped nonchalantly from the edge of his shorts' pocket, mimicking his grandfather's stance. Madame Pamier moved through to the shop to join her husband and Beth excused herself and sauntered towards the window to exchange a few words with the property owner. Returning to the shop to collect her diary, she found herself face to face with Delacroix.

"So, this is the new business venture, is it?" His loud and harsh Canadian tone brought a guarded hush to the various conversations. She glanced at Jacques, who bristled and crossed his arms in front of his chest. The welcome glass of wine for this particular visitor remained on the counter. Everyone from the village exchanged looks with each other but no one spoke to, nor acknowledged, the very tardy latecomer. Beth shifted her thinking to English and broke the silence.

"Thank you for coming, Mr Delacroix, and yes, this is my new place of work. I would also like to remind you that this is France and here we speak French." She moved over to the counter, collected a glass of champagne and handed it to him.

"No-one seems to like my Canadian accent, Beth." He grinned and took the wine. "And it's good to use our mother-tongue when we can, don't you think?"

Beth took a step back. "It's Madame Samuels, Mr Delacroix, and please help yourself to *canapés* and join the rest of my guests."

Delacroix scooped up a handful of food and turned away.

"That man is insufferable," Beth whispered, as she joined Jacques behind the counter. She handed him her empty glass. "I don't know why I bothered to invite him." Her attention focussed on Delacroix, she watched him as he moved towards Monsieur and Madame Pamier, both of whom turned away, suddenly engaged in conversation about one of the old cameras on display.

Jacques slipped his hand around Beth's waist and pulled her close. "Forget it," he whispered. "Delacroix's just an ill-mannered bore."

"Monsieur and Madame Mancelle," announced Delacroix as he moved towards them. "The parents of the now famous boy on the banner. Pierre, isn't it?"

Marie nodded and moved over to Jacques and Beth.

"Thank you for inviting us, and Martin and I will see you here a week on Saturday, as arranged." She went to the entrance to the back room and beckoned to Pierre.

The departure of Marie, Martin and their son became the beginning of a steady, but intermittent, flow towards the door of the majority of the attendees. An hour later, there remained only her business neighbours from both sides of the short street, Delacroix, and Jacques, steadfastly carrying out his work as *maître d'*.

Beth flicked through the pages of her desk diary. "Seventeen bookings, Jacques. That's a great afternoon's work, I think."

"And reason to open this final bottle of champagne," he said. As he eased out the cork and poured her a glass, Delacroix emerged from the studio. Jacques continued to fill the next couple of glasses, whilst keeping one eye on the

Canadian.

"I can add another booking if there's room for one," said Delacroix, a wide-open smile on his face.

Beth made another mental shift to English and checked the pages of the diary.

"I've got a slot tomorrow at 11.30 if it's just a studio portrait that you want."

"No, it's a bit more complicated than that."

Jacques stopped pouring the wine and leaned back against the wall and waited.

"That wine looking for an owner or is it just for decoration?"

"Please help yourself," said Beth. "This complication, Mr Delacroix, how can I help?"

"Now that the work on the farmhouse is more or less complete I'm going to be living here permanently. I'm in the process of transferring all my businesses and assets to France, and I need to start making new and more prestigious connections over here. I've secured the opportunity to be interviewed over the phone by a journalist from Paris for a business magazine next week. They were going to send a photographer down here to get some shots to go with the article, but I told them there was someone local who could do it for them." He took a mouthful of wine and grinned at Jacques. Turning his back on him he took a step towards Beth. "I was hoping you could find some time to come to the farmhouse and take some shots for me?"

Beth glanced at Jacques and saw the question in his eyes. "What sort of shots?"

"The angle the journalist is going to take is, kind of, a bad boy come good, if you know what I mean? She wants an old photo of me as a child along with some of me now in my new office environment, the remodelled farmhouse, and maybe a couple of the area around here." He finished the champagne and handed the glass to Jacques. "Thanks, Jack."

"Photos of the house, your office and the area I can do, but I'm not sure how I can help with the first requirement."

Delacroix reached into his jacket and pulled out his wallet from which he extracted a small, badly creased black and white photograph. "My parents weren't big on photographs and this is the only one I have," he said as he handed it to her.

Beth examined the picture carefully, turning it over to see if there was a studio stamp. But it was blank apart from a hand-written date of July 1969 and the last couple of letters of another word. She examined the right-hand edge and realised it had been torn very neatly.

"Do you or anyone else in the family still have the negative?"

"I don't, and there isn't really anyone else to ask."

Beth looked at him and saw what she thought was sadness in his bright blue eyes. She recognised the loneliness that comes with the loss of someone close and in that moment, her animosity towards him began to dwindle.

"I'm sorry," she said, her response automatic. "Sorry... um, the negative would have been useful to get another copy of the photo but if this is all there is, then I can work with that. It just means that I'll have to create a digital copy."

"And the damage? Can that be fixed?" He reached around her and helped himself to another glass of champagne.

"Oh, yes. Of course it can, and I would have done that anyway. It'll probably take me about a day, maybe a little more, to put right. But you do realise, don't you, that the magazine will have the capability to do that for you?"

"Yeah, I guess so, but I won't be able to see it before it's published if I let them do that, and I may not get it back. I'd rather you did the work."

Beth glanced at Jacques. "We'll be in Messandrierre at the weekend as usual." He nodded his agreement. "How does Saturday at two sound for the shots of the house?"

"That suits me fine," he said.

"I'll hang onto this," she said indicating the old photograph. "I can probably get most of the work on it done tomorrow. I can let you have it back when I come to do the shots of the house."

"Sounds like a plan." He gulped down the remainder of his wine and put the glass on the counter. "See you Saturday." He turned and strode out of the shop.

The last to leave, Beth closed the door on Delacroix and turned the lock.

"A wonderful day," she said. "A successful day too." She moved across to Jacques and put her arms around his waist. "Thank you for being here and for the ear-rings. They are perfect."

"I know," he said, "and you can thank me properly, later."

friday, june 17ᵗʰ, morning

As had become his habit of late when he needed a few moments away from his desk, Jacques stood at the windows of his office scrutinising the people and vehicles as they moved on the road below. He had been very much aware of the absence of his tail whilst with Beth at the opening of her shop the previous afternoon. That absence had concerned him. As he scanned the street below he calculated that he hadn't seen his tail for almost twenty-four hours, and that realisation caused him to worry.

Didier joined him. "The report of my interview yesterday with the cleaner who worked for Vauclain is on your desk, Jacques."

Jacques nodded. "Thanks. Any sign of your tail today?"

"No."

"Keep looking, Didier. They want something and whatever it is, they believe we have it or know about it. Considering their connections, they are not going to disappear, just like that."

"OK. I'll stay vigilant."

Satisfied that he had not, as yet, identified a new tail, Jacques relaxed a little and strolled back to his desk.

"What was your impression of the cleaner?" He quickly glanced through the report.

Didier settled himself in the chair opposite Jacques. "A busybody. Far too talkative for her own good, but an excellent witness. She recognised Berger immediately when I showed her the photo. Berger was a regular visitor to the house, and he and Vauclain often argued, and she was insistent it was always about money. She knew who Antoine Beaufort was, too. He had been to Vauclain's house before.

Only once on his own, as far as she could remember, but on a number of occasions with Chef Berger."

"She might remember Beaufort being there once, but that doesn't mean it was the only time he was there alone with Vauclain."

"Agreed," said Didier. "But there's something else. She said the destruction of the restaurant in Montbel was not the first time this had happened to Vauclain. There was a property on the outskirts of Orléans, about ten years ago, that he had inherited. It was in a dilapidated state and, according to the cleaner, he arranged for it to be torched so that he could collect the insurance, rebuild and sell at a significant profit."

"That sounds exactly like the rumour that Gaston from the bar in Messandrierre repeated to me about the fire at the place in Montbel. Are you sure she hasn't confused the two events?"

"No, she was very clear, and she didn't come across to me as someone who could be easily confused. And I've checked. There was an old property in Orléans that did burn down. It was reported in the papers at the time, and there was an investigation. Vauclain was one of three members of the family who inherited a share."

"And that would also put Vauclain in or around Orléans at the same time that Chef Berger was there, along with Beaufort. Was this picked up during the investigation into the Montbel incident?"

Didier shook his head. "The cleaner did report her suspicions to the police here in Mende. She could even tell me what day of the week it was when she came into the station. A statement was taken, but no one contacted her again. I've checked with my old colleagues, and any connection between the two incidents was ruled out because Luc Nowak was a juvenile in custody at the time of the fire in Orléans. He was in the middle of serving an eight-month sentence."

"And what were Madame's views on what might have happened to the insurance pay-out following the fire in

Montbel?"

Didier chuckled. "A little fantastical, at best. But she did keep reiterating one particular point throughout my interview with her, not just when I asked about the money. Vauclain lived beyond his means and had a very expensive woman that he kept secret—"

"But not from her?"

"Not quite. Madame walked in on the two of them having breakfast together. She wasn't supposed to be at his house until after lunch that particular day, but had gone in early because she wanted to remove the nets and get them in the wash."

Jacques grinned. "And I'm supposed to accept that's the truth rather than a story to cover her nosiness?"

"She was adamant, Jacques. Perhaps a little too adamant!"

"Do we know who this secret woman is?"

"Not by name, no. But I think that old postcard from Cannes that we found with the phone number on the back is connected. According to the cleaner, the woman is married and has a villa just outside Cannes. We know the number on the back of the card is no longer active, but there is the number in Vauclain's contacts list ending 4591 which is still active and still unaccounted for. I have left another message but I've indicated that we know about her connection to Vauclain. Maybe this time I'll get a response."

"OK, and thanks."

"One more thing. Last week, you were asking about who might know we are looking for Beaufort."

"Yes."

Didier picked up the report, turned to the last page and placed a copy of a newspaper article in front of Jacques. "That's Antoine Beaufort in 2009," he said pointing to a tall man in a white shirt, wearing a dark apron and cap and carrying a large two-handled pan.

"Can we get the original or a copy sent over?"

"A copy is already on the way to us. I also spoke to the journalist. This shot was one of a number taken about a month before the fire. The names of the people in the background weren't taken because Chef Berger insisted that he didn't want his kitchens or his staff to be used for the article. Instead, they took some other shots of Berger in the restaurant and in his office and they used one of those. This shot was put into the archives until the editor pulled it out for this particular article because it had not been used before. The journalist subsequently sold a revised and expanded version of this article with this photograph and two others to a magazine that is available all over the country."

"That means anyone looking for Beaufort would have known he was here, before the fire," said Jacques. "Good work, Didier. I think it's time we went to see Chef Berger again, but unannounced, this time. Do we know what his working hours are today?"

"I'll check," said Didier as he slipped out of Jacques' office.

Settled in his chair, Jacques began to read through all of the detail of the report, making notes in his own notebook as he did so. A few moments later, Didier popped his head around the door.

"Berger is on duty until about 19.00 tonight," he said. "He will oversee the final preparations for the evening service and then go home. He's not working again until Monday, and it is normal for him not to remain in his rooms at the hotel when he has a whole weekend off."

"Which, if we're lucky, might mean he will be at Les Alpiers." Jacques thought for a moment. *And that gives me plenty of time to rattle him.* "You and I will handle this ourselves."

Didier nodded and disappeared.

Jacques glanced at his watch and then picked up his desk phone to call Beth.

***

Beth had been busy all morning with the sales generated by her online customers. Distracted by the formal opening of the shop the previous afternoon had meant that responses for online orders had been temporarily neglected. There were also a couple of contacts who required photographic work, and those appointments were quickly and easily dealt with by phone and slotted into her diary.

The remainder of the outstanding work was dealing with the online sales. She was particularly pleased to see that some of her mounted photographs were finally beginning to sell. There were three payments in for pieces of photographic equipment that had originally been Old Thierry's. She was careful to allocate those funds to a separate and specific bank account that she wanted to use to finance a photographic competition in the following year in memory of the old photographer. Her hope was that the competition would become an annual event. She was just finishing the packaging of a telephoto lens for a customer in Australia when her phone rang. It was Jacques.

"Hi... What? No, of course not..." She listened and then checked her watch. "I hadn't realised it was coming up to lunchtime. I've had a lot to catch up on after yesterday, and I haven't even started work on Delacroix's photo yet... No, I don't mind. It'll give me a chance to work through... Yes, I'll go straight to Messandrierre after I've closed the shop and meet you there tonight, then... OK. Bye."

The bottom menu bar on her computer said it was almost 11.00 and she still needed another hour or so to finish her work packing and wrapping the last few items that had been sold through her website. *If I hurry, I should be able to get this done and the packages to the post office before it closes for lunch.* Her resolution made, she set about her task with renewed vigour.

friday, june 17ᵗʰ, lunchtime

Jacques had just completed reading Didier's report and was in the process of filing it when Maxim appeared at the door.

"A visitor for you," he said, standing back.

"Bruno, this is an unexpected surprise. I was just about to leave for lunch." The investigating magistrate's demeanour caused Jacques' welcoming smile to dissipate almost immediately. He gestured to the seat on the opposite side of his desk. "What can I do for you?"

Pelletier slumped down, a world-weary look on his face. "I have something for you," he said as he delved into his briefcase and pulled out a slim brown file. "But you didn't get this from me, if anyone asks. I just wanted you to be forewarned."

Jacques nodded and took the file and laid it out on his desk. He and Pelletier had worked on this basis before, and they both knew that they could trust each other implicitly. He recognised immediately what the file was. Opening it, he skimmed through the various pages. There was only one thing he needed to know. As he read the pathologist's report, hoping for a clear answer, his face showed nothing but confusion. Just to be sure he had understood correctly, he read the relevant paragraphs again.

"How is that possible?"

Pelletier remained tight-lipped.

Jacques stared at the report. He flipped the card cover of the file shut, a resigned look on his face. "This means that you'll want all our papers and copies of all our interview reports."

Pelletier nodded. "And we will need to interview you and anyone else who is, or has been, involved, Jacques."

"When can I expect your formal visit to sequester our papers?"

"Would Monday afternoon give you enough time to get everything together for us?"

Jacques nodded. "Thanks, Bruno." They shook hands and the magistrate collected his file of papers and left.

"Damn it," Jacques muttered under his breath as he considered how he should handle the rest of his day's work. It occurred to him that perhaps he should postpone his current plans for interviewing Berger again that evening. But as soon as that thought had entered his conscious mind, he banished it. *I've got until Monday. And it was only a best match for the partial print*. He checked his watch, collected his jacket and bag, and strode into the main office.

"I'm not meeting Beth for lunch today," he announced as he breezed in. "Pelletier's visit has left us with an added complication, which I'll explain later, but I still want our plans for this afternoon and this evening to go ahead. I'll eat at home, and meet you back here at 14.00. I'll come back on the bike."

Didier nodded and added, as Jacques disappeared out of the door, "OK, and I'll do the same and come back in the car."

Jacques took the stairs down to the ground floor. Cautious still, he checked the street before he left the building. He darted across the main road, dodging the traffic, and then threaded his way through the narrow, and less frequented, streets until he arrived in the suburb of Merle. Having doubled-back on his route a couple of times, he felt sure he was alone when he approached *Hirondelle*, his apartment building. He let himself in, collected the post from the box and then climbed the stairs two at a time until he reached the first floor landing, and stopped. He remained absolutely still, listening and waiting. There was nothing but silence. Five minutes later, he was letting himself into the apartment.

Certain that the door was securely locked, he dropped his keys in the dish on the small table in the vestibule and walked into the *salon* and straight across the living space to the dining area and kitchen. He didn't notice that there was something different about one of a series of Beth's framed photographs on the wall to his left. It was the picture just above his eye level, and it was fractionally out of line.

Hanging his jacket over the back of one of the chairs, he pulled it out slightly and placed his bag on the seat. Turning to go to the kitchen he took two steps and froze.

***

Shortly after Jacques left the office, Didier collected his jacket and his morning newspaper and exited the building to return home for lunch. He took the lift to the basement car park, let himself out through the code-locked meshed gate and walked briskly down the narrow road that ran behind the office. His route took him close to the cathedral, into rue Soubeyran, where he had bought his newspaper that morning and past the *boulangerie* where he called in to collect his bread. Today, he had one other establishment to visit: the post office to drop off a couple of business letters, before taking his usual walking route out of the city centre and back to his first floor apartment overlooking the river Lot. Not that there was much of a view of the river from his place. The riverbank at that point was shaded with well-established trees, but from his balcony, in summer, he could hear the water flow, and it was a peaceful and cool place to sit.

As he turned into his street his work mobile phone pinged to let him know that a text message had arrived. The sound was specific and pertained to only one kind of message. He stopped immediately and pulled his phone out of the pocket on his white cotton shirt. The message was from Jacques and contained a single coded word.

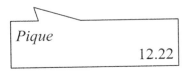

Pique

12.22

I've got to get off the street, he thought. *Fast.* He checked his surroundings. No one else was visible. Breaking into a sprint, he ran to the top of the road and took the steps down to the riverbank. There was a path that ran between his apartment block and the river, and he knew he would be able to see the windows of his apartment. It would be obvious if someone had tried to access his property from the balcony. Everything seemed to be exactly as he had left it. He carried on along the path a little way until he reached the gate that separated the tenement from the river path. As he was about to key-in the entrance code, he noticed that the gate wasn't properly secured.

"That's been tampered with," he muttered to himself as he examined the lock closely. There was no doubt in his mind about that.

The rear entrance to the building was just to his left. Using his key, he let himself in. He took the stairs to his floor and before he walked onto his landing, he stopped and checked to see if anyone else was about. From his vantage point, he could see the door to his apartment. Approaching with caution, he slipped the key in the lock as silently as possible and carefully turned it to release the barrels. *OK so far.* He pushed the door open slightly and peered inside. Everything seemed to be in place. With the door closed behind him, he could not be sure what, or possibly who, was waiting for him. The place was silent. Only the familiar chime for the half hour of the mantle clock that his wife had cherished was audible. He pushed open the door on his right. Anyone standing behind it would be reflected in the mirror of the dressing table opposite, and he would be able to see that reflection through the gap at the hinges. No one was there. He pushed the door wide open and marched in. The room was clear, but he still checked the wardrobes.

Continuing his check of the other rooms, he finally reached his dining-kitchen area and took a deep breath. As his eyes worked their way round the room he felt another moment of rising panic. He stood stock still, gazing at the table.

It was a familiar tactic. He knew that. He'd seen it dozens of times before, just not in his property. It unnerved him.

He placed his bread and his newspaper on the worktop. Reaching for the plastic evidence gloves that he kept under the sink, he picked up the folded newspaper that lay in the centre of the table. It was that morning's paper. His name was scrawled on it in the top right corner. Comparing the writing with that on the copy he had just set down on the worktop, it was obvious that is was the same script. *Same colour ink.*

"Probably the same pen," he said to himself. He took out his personal mobile and texted Jacques. His message containing a single coded word. Jacques would know that he was OK.

He removed his jacket and hung it on a chair. His police training taking control, he undertook a systematic and detailed search of the whole place, looking for anything that may have been left by the intruder. The search provided no clues. Nothing was missing and, apart from the newspaper left in the centre of the table, whoever had been in his place had left no other trace. Nor was there anything to suggest why they had been there. Didier assumed it was the current investigation. But who? Who was so determined to let them know they were watching? And watching closely?

Didier lifted the receiver on his landline and was about to dial his son's number when he stopped. Instead, he checked the phone for any possible electronic bugs that might have been placed there. It took a minute to find what he was looking for. He removed the device and dropped it into his shirt pocket.

Taking his personal mobile from the pocket in his shirt, he moved out onto the balcony and closed the windows behind him. This time he dialled the number he really wanted.

"Sorry to interrupt your lunch, son, but I need your help... Not over the phone... Yes, it's urgent… Thanks. Just get here as soon as you can."

***

As she made her way back from the Post office Beth contemplated something to eat. Making lunch the main meal of her day was still a habit she found trying. Meeting Jacques regularly, when they were both in Mende during the week, was something she always enjoyed. Eating out by herself had never been appealing, not even when she was living in England. Faced with the prospect of eating alone today tempered her appetite. She glanced over at the *pâtisserie* across from her studio as she made her way along the street to her own shop doorway. Her mind was soon made up. A sandwich and one of their *amandine* was all that was required and, she reasoned, it would give her some precious time to do some of the work on Delacroix's photograph. Her purchases made, she dashed across the road and let herself in.

Back at her computer, she started work on the photo and became engrossed. Soon, she had a new digital copy of the black and white picture of a boy, aged about nine or ten, stood in front of an ironwork fence displayed on her computer screen. She sat back and shook her head at the monitor.

"Whoever you were, you had a serious case of camera shake when you took this shot." She clicked through her menu options until she found what she wanted. Incrementally, she sharpened the shot until she was satisfied. The photo returned to normal size when she clicked to zoom-out. She picked up the original and examined the right edge closely. *I wonder who, or what, has been so very carefully torn out of this picture.* Her mind began to bounce from questions to possible answers as she took the first bite from her sandwich. Whilst she came up with what she thought could be plausible explanations, she always came back to the same unanswerable question of why?

At twenty past one, her sandwich barely touched, she finally stopped to make herself a coffee. But that didn't mean that she took a break. As she munched the rest of her way through the baguette, she circled the mouse around the picture, zooming in on the remaining damaged areas, making a full assessment of exactly how much more there was to do. *Hmm, that crease will be a bit difficult to take out.*

An hour or so later, her coffee cold and half-drunk, she had the basic work completed. Now, she needed to concentrate on the complex and detailed fixes required. She decided to work on the torn edge first and zoomed in and then methodically began to repair the tiny splinters of change in surface colour. Beth gradually worked upwards along the edge until her task was complete. She took a deep breath and stretched.

The arrival of a young woman and her mother became a welcome distraction as she took details of a booking for a wedding in May of the following year.

Turning her attention to the photograph again, she carefully worked away at the crease until she had obliterated every last trace. All that remained to be fixed were the three original white edges that had once formed the border and she cropped these out. Puzzled, she zoomed in on the top right hand corner and realised that there was an item in the background that she hadn't particularly taken notice of before. It was a sign of some sort, or a part of a sign just above the boy's left shoulder. A road sign or a street name, were her first thoughts. She peered at it. *Concentrate.* Obeying her own command, she copied the top right-hand corner of the photo and saved it to her hard drive and then went back to her repair work. She could look at that corner separately when she had more time. Now, she needed to reframe the whole picture and that took just a few clicks of the mouse. Her very last task was to brighten the picture by adjusting the contrast and balancing the shadow and the light. Everything completed, she saved her work and then printed a replacement photograph. As the printer in the studio whirred into action, she went back to the photo and focussed on the boy's head and shoulders. Using that as the centre of a second picture she cropped out the background, reframed the picture, saved it and sent a copy to print. Her last task was to save all three versions of the picture to a CD to pass onto Delacroix the next day. As she waited for the printer to complete its task, she began to pick up the messages and enquiries that had arrived through her website since she last checked.

friday, june 17th, afternoon

In the quiet of the boardroom on the fourth floor of the Vaux Consulting building, Didier and Jacques were sharing an array of charcuterie. Neither had eaten at home as originally planned. Both, having completed a search of their respective properties, had met with Philippe Chauvin, the IT Director, and his deputy. It was part of the protocol that Jacques had instituted when he had set up an agreed security procedure should any one of his investigators, himself or any part of his team, find themselves in danger or compromised during an investigation. Philippe and his deputy had already swept the room for listening devices before Jacques arrived. It was clean.

"I stopped off at the newsagents' on my way back here," said Didier once they had the Boardroom to themselves. "Whoever took my paper this morning went in just as the shop opened. He said he was a friend and was collecting the paper on my behalf. The owner said he was of average height, brown hair, and light jacket. That was all I could get. It also explains why, when I called in at my usual time, the owner's wife couldn't find my paper and had to take one off the display for me, which she then scribbled my name on as usual."

"And what about your apartment?"

"Same result as you. Just the one listening device, nothing taken but I'm certain the place was searched. My son is house sitting for me, and I've got the locksmith coming this afternoon."

"The ruse they used to access my place was a complaint of a water leak from the apartment below mine and their calling card was a cup and saucer set out in the centre of the worktop in the kitchen. I checked with the concierge and got nothing of any use as a description either. These men are clever, Didier. They mean business. I'm also certain my place was searched and it was very carefully done. Things not in exactly the right place, or at least that's what they want you to think. And the listening device was behind one of Beth's photos. I think it was meant to be found."

Didier nodded as he helped himself to some *rosette* and another piece of bread. "What's next, Jacques?"

"We know Chef Berger will be busy at the hotel until this evening so we don't need to be watching that place until around 18.00." He glanced at his watch, "That gives us time to put pressure on Madame Beaufort to be completely honest with us."

"OK. My car's parked under our building. I'll check in with Philippe on my way down that a new set of phones is ready for us, and I'll meet you there."

"Twenty minutes," said Jacques.

Jacques waited in the entrance hall for Madame Beaufort's assistant to return and take him to her. Didier stayed outside in the car. Jacques had given him very clear instructions about what he had to do.

Some minutes later, and Jacques found himself in Madame's sitting room on the first floor, a glass of iced water on the coffee table in front of him.

"You told me, Madame, that your son, Antoine, left after an argument. My enquiries now lead me to believe that there was more to it than that." He showed her his copy of the family picture she had on her desk. "That boy there," he said pointing to the child with the blond hair stood next to his mother, "is your son, Antoine. But he's not Charles Beaufort's son, is he?"

Henriette maintained a stony silence. Her breathing, as shallow as it was, remained steady, but her stare was as icy and unforgiving as the storm that had hit the valley one week ago.

"Is that the real reason that Antoine left, Madame? Not

some family argument, but the discovery that Charles Beaufort was not his real father?" Jacques waited but his patience was rewarded with only silence.

"I've had someone check the details of Antoine's birth, and he was christened Antoine Charles Maximilian. That's quite a name to live up to, isn't it?"

Still she said nothing.

"Antoine is your father's name. And the name Charles... Could that be for Monsieur Beaufort, or Antoine's grandfather? Then we have this third name, Maximilian."

"It's just a name, Monsieur Forêt. A very pleasing name to me."

"But it's not a family name, is it? Not in the de Garmeaux or the Beaufort family. We've checked."

The glimmer of a wry smile flitted across her face. "That's because I chose it on a whim."

Jacques pressed on. "We've discovered some other interesting things about you too, Madame." He placed in front of her a copy of an article from a society magazine in 1950. "I found this photograph particularly interesting, Madame. Here you are, at a 25th birthday party, with one of this regions most prosperous heiresses at the time and her *fiancé*. According to the reporter, Charles Beaufort is the second man in the photo. The reporter goes on to speculate that Charles was expected to propose to you and that the announcement would be the next society event of the year. Odd that it should take you until 1963 to make up your mind to accept him."

For the first time since he arrived, Madame Beaufort looked away. "My marriage was one of convenience. You can't begin to understand how things were done back then. Where money and property were involved, a lot of marriages were for convenience."

"But that's something else that I now know, Madame. For you, there was no property, was there? You call your marriage one of convenience, but I think it was a necessity. It's a little difficult to call a three kilo baby premature." Jacques pushed across the table a copy of the announcement of the birth in the newspaper. "At that time, considering your family connections, an unmarried mother…"

Henriette shot him a glance and he knew he'd hit a raw nerve. "Get out! Your work for me is finished," she spat out her words.

Jacques ploughed on. "Your family own an apartment in Passy that is currently valued at around €5 million. Not that you or your sister or any of your children or grandchildren will see a single *centime.* Your grandfather made sure of that, didn't he? Purchasing that apartment when it was newly built as a business asset rather than a family home, made sure of that, didn't it? And it has remained as a business asset for de Garmeaux Associates, the current name for your family's various business interests, hasn't it?"

Henriette's breathing became ragged. Jacques wondered if he'd pushed her too far. But he wouldn't stop. I've only got until Monday, he thought.

"When was the last time you set foot in that grace-and-favour home in which you were born, Madame?"

Henriette's demeanour changed and a tiredness crossed her face. Jacques thought he saw the beginning of a tear but she looked down and shook her head before he could be sure.

"A long time ago," she said. "It was all such a long time ago. Do you know what it feels like to be possessed? To have your life ordered for you." She looked at him, her stare cold and hard. "I was last in that apartment in Passy when I was fifteen. I haven't set foot in there since."

Jacques took a sip of his water and waited. Henriette seemed to age before his eyes. He broke the silence. "Why was that, Madame?"

"There are some things that can never be spoken of, Monsieur Forêt." Henriette wheeled her chair over to her desk and unlocked a narrow drawer in the centre at the front. Jacques watched as she retrieved something and then returned to where he was sitting. The exertion had winded her and she reached for her oxygen and took half-a-dozen deep breaths.

"Antoine is my son, and Charles was his father in name only," she said. "It was an agreement that we came to. This was Antoine's real father. He was the only man I ever truly loved." She placed a small black and white photograph on the table and pushed it across to him. "They say every picture tells a story, Monsieur, and that one will tell you everything you need to know."

Jacques glanced down and saw a serious-looking young man. "Thank you," he said as he picked up the picture and secured it to his papers.

"Take care with what you find, Monsieur." Henriette turned her chair away. "There are some secrets that need to go with me to my grave. Now, please leave me and find my son."

Jacques watched silently as she wheeled herself across to the open windows and out onto the balcony.

Driving back to Mende, Didier did most of the talking with Jacques responding only when absolutely required.

"Madame's flunky was certain that the cookery book was posted in Le Puy. He no longer has the wrapping that it came in, but he is as certain of where it was posted as he is that the address label was typed and addressed to the old nanny."

"Which suggests that it must have come from Berger and yet again, he knows more than he's telling us."

Didier moved over a lane to pass a couple of trucks. "He particularly remembers the book because he did not recognise the name on the package when it arrived and wondered if it had come to the wrong address. When he checked with Monsieur Jean-Charles Beaufort about the package, he was left in no doubt that the matter was not for his attention. Jean-Charles took the book and all the packaging." Didier fell silent as he negotiated some more slow moving traffic.

"What explanation did Jean-Charles give Madame's assistant for taking charge of the book?"

"Just that, the old nanny was very dear to his mother and that something like the book would cause the old lady great heartache. And with her health in severe decline...etc., etc. I then moved onto more general enquiries about the family and..." Didier paused as he checked his mirror in anticipation of changing lanes again. "He's a very loyal employee, Jacques. Whilst he wouldn't be specific, he did hint at difficulties in the past. Those where his chosen words to describe what I concluded, from the hints he gave me, must have been a family rift that began long before Antoine Beaufort was born."

Jacques nodded as he thought about his conversation and the photo that Madame had given him. A photo that he had barely had time to look at before he was asked to leave. Didier remained silent as he drove through the traffic in the centre of Mende and threaded his way around the one-way system and into his designated parking space in the underground car park of the Vaux Investigations building.

"We've got about an hour before we need to leave to watch the hotel for Berger," said Jacques as they made their way to his office. "I've got something that Madame Beaufort gave me, and I think there is a whole new line of enquiry that we need to follow up on urgently."

"I'll get Maxim and Amélie to deal with that."

Jacques dropped his bag on his desk and slumped down in his chair. He took a deep breath and retrieved the new evidence and laid it out on his desk. The photo was small and just a headshot. The young man was wearing a shirt and tie and looked prosperous. He turned it over and found an inscription on the back, which he automatically translated in his mind as he read it. *Max, short for Maximilian. So Maximilian was the name of Antoine's real father.*

He looked up and smiled at Didier. "It's not much to go on, but this is a photo of Antoine's biological father. Madame did admit that he wasn't Charles Beaufort's son, as we suspected. We've got a first name, which is Maximilian, but she wouldn't give me anything else." Jacques handed the photo to Didier.

"I'll see what we can do but tracing someone just from a photo isn't going to be easy," Didier looked at the picture. "And this looks very old."

"I know, but we haven't got much time. I'm authorising overtime for the full weekend, and if Maxim needs the photo to be enhanced then tell him to talk to Beth directly."

Didier nodded and left. Propped up against the monitor on Jacques' desk was a note from Amélie directing him to look at some new information along with the file details. He logged on and clicked straight through. As he read, his mind worked. He sat staring at the screen for a few moments, the words just drifting before his eyes, his mind slotting the pieces of the puzzle together. But there was a detail he was missing. Something he knew was stored at the back of his mind but just could not recall.

Wait a minute, what was it she said today? He took his mind back to the conversation with Henriette. *She was fifteen when she last…* Madame, what have you done, he thought as realisation dawned. *We've been looking in the wrong place.* He quickly jotted down some notes and raced through to the general office.

"Amélie, I need you to make some enquiries for me. And I need all of this before Monday." He spread his note on her desk and took her through the work.

friday, june 17th, evening

Jacques was waiting for Chef Berger to leave Hotel Claustres as planned. The evening was warm again, and Jacques wondered if another thunderstorm might be on the way. The streets were almost empty of the workers who had populated them during the day, and the bistros and *cafés* were beginning to fill with new customers. At a little after seven, Berger's car emerged from the underground car park. Shrinking back into the shadow, Jacques watched to see which route he would take out of the city. At the junction with avenue Foch, Berger turned left and headed up towards the inner ring road. Jacques phoned Didier who was waiting, as agreed, on boulevard Henri Bourrillon.

"He's on the move and heading your way... OK... Good... Keep me updated."

Jacques walked back to his office, collected his helmet, and bag from where he had left them at security on the ground floor and made his way to where he had parked his bike. Helmet on and earpiece plugged into his phone, he set off to follow the route that Berger had taken. As expected, the chef was making his way to Les Alpiers. Jacques stuck to the speed limits. He wanted to give Berger as much time as possible to get settled.

Still listening to Didier's running commentary on the route, Jacques pulled off the main road and onto the D901. He knew he would be with Didier in about twenty minutes and decided to take his time.

On the outskirts of the village, he parked up and walked to where his colleague was parked. Just as he settled himself in the passenger seat, his personal phone pinged to let him know a text had arrived. Jacques retrieved his phone.

***

For Beth the drive from Mende was quiet. The traffic was concentrated in the city as usual, and once she had crossed the river and was climbing out of the valley, the only other vehicles were a couple of logging trucks and a speeding motorist probably anxious to get home to his wife before she became suspicious of his lateness. Beth smiled.

The evening sun was playing on the mountainside on her right as she approached Badaroux where she stopped to pick up some bread. The final few kilometres drifted by as she drove on autopilot, her mind more interested in the colours of the scenery. *Think I'll bring the camera out here tomorrow or Sunday. Hopefully Jacques won't mind.* She glanced at the clock on the dash to note the time. A passing motorist honked his horn at her and then shook his fist as he raced by. She pulled her car back into her own lane and then had to correct her steering again because she was about to veer onto the verge. *Concentrate.*

Without any further distractions, she pulled into Messandrierre and hairpinned left onto the D6 and up the slope to her chalet where she left the car in front of the garage. Letting herself in, she dropped her bag on the bottom step of the spiral staircase and went straight through to the kitchen with the bread. As she passed the nook she halted.

"Jacques?" There was no reply. "Jacques... Must have been and gone again."

She shrugged and moved over to the table, it was set for one. A single flower from the garden in a small glass vase she kept in a cupboard in the kitchen had been placed to one side. In the space between the cutlery a copy of Gaston and Marianne's take-away menu. She smiled. *How do you always manage to surprise me, Jacques?*

She moved around the small table to the French windows to open them and let in the air. When she tried to release the lock she realised the windows were already unsecured. *Oh Jacques, that was silly. Very thoughtful about the table, but silly not to lock up properly before you left again, tut.* She pushed the windows wide open and a breath of warm air, carrying with it the scent of the pines and the mountains, filled the room.

Leaving the bread on the table, she went to get her phone from her bag. She sent a text to Jacques.

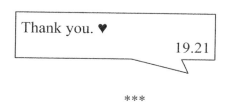

Thank you. ♥

19.21

***

In Les Alpiers, Didier updated Jacques as they waited in the car.

"He's inside. He came here direct from the hotel and appears to be alone."

Jacques, having retrieved a message, stared at his phone in bafflement. It didn't make sense. He scrolled back through his messages, wondering if he'd missed something.

"Everything all right, Jacques?"

"Not sure, but I think I need to speak to Beth." He got out of the car, walked a little way down the slope and called her.

"Hi, it's me..." He listened as she described her surprise on arrival at the chalet. In response he tried to keep his voice light. "All part of the service, Madame... The windows? Did I? Sorry... Didier was waiting for me... Beth, this job is going to take longer than I originally thought. I'll be another two, maybe three hours yet, so why don't you spend the evening with Marianne and Gaston at the restaurant instead. Tell Gaston I'll pay when... OK. I just thought it might be better for you that's... OK." He ended the call.

Jacques sprinted back to the car and got in. "We need 24-hour surveillance on the chalet. Our friends from earlier today have been there too, and Beth is alone. I've suggested to her that she goes to the village restaurant tonight to eat, but she's decided to eat by herself. She's got some work to complete before tomorrow, she says."

"Does she know that our watchers have been to the chalet?"

"No. They laid out the table in the nook for one. She assumed I'd done it, and I let her think that." The questioning look in Didier's eyes was not lost on Jacques.

"I don't want to worry her, Didier. And I think they must have come in through the French windows at the back."

"Jacques, how did they know she would be there alone?"

Jacques frowned and thought for a moment. "My call. It can only have been my call this morning, which means my room is compromised."

Didier pulled out his phone. "You watch Berger," he said as he got out of the car. "I'll get the surveillance in place and get a sweep of our offices organised as well."

Jacques nodded and focussed his attention on the windows of the old house. He had to keep his head clear but worrying thoughts were bombarding his mind. *They won't come back. It's just a tactic. It's intimidation.*

"I won't be intimidated," he said aloud and kept on repeating it to himself. The verbalisation finally managing to banish the dark crowding thoughts.

A light was switched on in a room at the front of Chef Berger's property and Jacques checked his watch. A moment later, Didier got back in the car.

"Everything's in place," he said.

"Thanks. I think it's time for us to make our move," said Jacques.

A minute later, the two investigators were on Berger's front porch and Jacques rapped on the door and waited. When Jonnie Berger appeared in the open doorway, the smile on his face dropped instantly.

"Monsieur Forêt... Um, this isn't a very convenient time. I—"

"It is for us," Jacques interrupted him and took a step

forward. "And we won't keep you too long."

Berger looked from one to the other. "Come into my study," he said taking a couple of steps back and indicating a small room on his right.

"What do you want this time?" Berger strode across the room to the chair behind his desk and sat.

Jacques glanced around for a second chair. The walls of the room were lined with shelves on one side that contained a series of box files and bookshelves on the opposite wall. The only other seat was a small armchair over by the door that Didier was occupying, notebook and pen in hand, ready to make notes. Jacques remained standing.

"I wanted to talk to you about Étienne Vauclain," Jacques said. "I understand from his cleaning woman that you and he—"

"That woman has a habit of poking her nose into things that don't concern her." Berger glared at Jacques as he snapped out his statement.

Jacques continued, keeping his approach calm and measured. "She has told us that you and Vauclain were very close, Monsieur, and that you were a frequent visitor to his house in Montbel." He watched Berger intently. "I now understand that your business dealings with Vauclain were much more complex than you first suggested and that—"

"And that's were you and that senseless old gossip are wrong." Berger was on his feet, the colour of anger creeping up his neck and into his cheeks.

Jacques paused deliberately. He kept his face expressionless until he finally broke the silence.

"I didn't say who it was who told us your business dealings with Vauclain were complex, Monsieur." He pulled out a folded piece of paper from his jacket pocket, flattened it on the desk and turned it to face Berger.

"These payments here, Monsieur, from MPCC to Monsieur Vauclain. What were they for?"

Berger grabbed the document and screwed it up.

"I have other copies," said Jacques. "And that was only one copy of one of Vauclain's bank statements. They are others. They were all found at his property around the time of his murder. So I know the payments were made over a lengthy period of time." Jacques waited patiently, hands behind his back, as though he were in uniform and on duty again.

Berger met his glare with a lengthy stare. "There are many people that I deal with on a business footing. Vauclain was only one of them. I have regular outgoings to numerous suppliers for my catering business. It's not unusual, Monsieur Forêt."

He placed an undue emphasis on the word 'Monsieur'. "After all, that is what you are now, isn't it? Just plain Monsieur Forêt." Berger settled himself back in his chair, a smug grin on his face.

Jacques refused to be drawn. "Yes, you're right, but not wearing a uniform and no longer working as a policeman does not stop me from asking questions. MPCC is your catering business, is it not? The same business that supports your books. And, I presume, it is the same business that pays your supplier *Épicerie Giroux*. How is Madame Sylvie, by the way?"

"Get out of my house!" Berger was round the desk in a second. He grabbed Jacques by the jacket and tried to manhandle him across the room.

Didier sprang to his feet.

"That's enough," he shouted as he sought to free Jacques. "Enough!" Didier stood between the two of them.

Berger was breathing heavily. Jacques straightened his jacket. He stepped away.

"Something else that may interest you, Monsieur, is that the police now have a full forensics report from the scene of Vauclain's murder. They have a finger print that is of great interest to them." Jacques paused again and watched for Berger's reaction. The fingers of the Chef's right hand reached for a button on his shirt and began to pull at it.

Jacques moved to the door, stopped and turned. "Just one last thing, Chef Berger. If I can find evidence of regular payments of between €2,000 and €5,000, then so can

Investigating Magistrate Pelletier. I would also like to suggest that Magistrate Pelletier will be thinking along the same lines as me. Are these payments bona fide business transactions? Are they blackmail? Or are they a payoff in instalments for some very particular service rendered?"

The chef remained silent and unmoved.

"An alternative view would be to suggest that murder is a very convenient way to settle a bill or to rid oneself of a blackmailer. We'll see ourselves out, and you know where to find me if you want to talk."

***

The front door clicked shut. Berger moved over to the window and watched as Jacques and his colleague walked down the sloping stone path to the road. At the wide entrance to the farm, Jacques turned and looked back at the house for a moment. Berger stood his ground. The two men continued to watch each other until Berger slowly turned the blinds to blot out the last vestiges of the fading evening light.

He retrieved the copy of the bank statement and smoothed it straight. He carefully read through every entry on the page. "Hell fire!" He marched out of the study and into the large kitchen and dining area.

"He knows," Berger said, flinging the sheet of paper onto the table. "I think he knows or has guessed everything."

saturday, june 18th, 08.00am

In just his jeans, loafers, and a white cotton shirt, Jacques slipped out of the chalet in Messandrierre. The sky was bright blue and cloudless and the heat of the morning sun was tempered by the slow light breeze that meandered through the village. He made his way down to the end of the path. The car horn from the baker's van echoed across the valley as he waited for it to arrive. Another blast on the horn made Jacques look up. The baker had reached the fork in the road just above where he stood. From one of the hunting chalets across the road emerged an elderly lady, her grey hair still caught up in her curlers and her long pink dressing gown trailing around her slippered feet. They each nodded their morning greetings, and Jacques slowed his pace to give his elderly neighbour time to reach the baker and be served before him.

"Jacques, *bonjour*. Beth not with you this weekend?"

"*Bonjour*, and yes, Beth is here. I got up first. You should have some *croissants* and two *baguettes* for us."

The baker checked his order list, nodded and began putting the smaller items into a paper bag. "No *pain au chocolat*? I know Beth likes them, and I do have some left this morning?"

"I'd better take two of those as well." Jacques pulled a note out of his wallet. The baker exchanged the note for a second paper bag containing the extra pastries, counted out the change and handed that to Jacques.

"*À demain!*" He waved as he closed the van door and got behind the wheel. Jacques heard the vehicle accelerate down the road to the next stop, which was always Gaston's bar and restaurant.

Jacques pocketed his change and sprinted across the road and back to the chalet. As he walked in he could smell the fresh coffee on the hob and hear the clatter of crockery as Beth set out the cups, saucers, and plates.

"It's warm out. I was going to suggest we have breakfast outside," he said.

Beth reached into a drawer and took out a cloth. "OK, take that," she said as she tossed it across to him. "I'll bring everything else in a moment."

Jacques moved out of the kitchen and across to the nook where he would sometimes work when not in the office. He opened the windows into the room, reminding himself that he needed to get the locks changed. Unlocking the full-length shutters, he secured them back.

The patio overlooked a small terraced garden. Beyond that were some trees that separated their space from their neighbours and framed the high mountain peaks that surrounded the village. The cloth arranged, he returned to the kitchen.

"You've got a phone call," said Beth, her arm outstretched as she handed him the device.

"Hello... Chef Berger, *bonjour*... Yes... Meet you? Yes, I can do that..." He glanced at Beth. She shrugged in response. "I can't agree to that. I will... No... OK. Give me an hour, and I'll call you back."

Beth, her tray ladened with everything for breakfast, moved towards the patio. "I suppose that is work?" She put the tray on the table and began to set out the places.

"Yes. I put some pressure on Chef Berger last night and now he wants to talk." Jacques took his seat at the table and poured them both a cup of coffee.

"And when are you going to meet him?" Beth broke the end from her *croissant* and dunked it in her coffee.

Jacques smiled as he did the same. "Later today, probably, but I'm not happy with his terms. I need to talk to Didier first, and then I'll have to go into the office."

Beth cradled her cup. "OK. I had hoped we could both be here to talk to Marie about the music for the wedding, but that can wait."

Jacques sliced himself a chunk of bread. "Do you really need me for that? I'm sure you and Marie would make much better choices about music than I would." He grinned at her.

"Mmm. Your taste in music does leave a lot to be desired." She drained her coffee and poured a second cup. "You go to work and I'll sort everything out with Marie. I doubt that we'll be making any final decisions today anyway, so there'll be other chances for you to have your say."

"I can live with that," he said, a broad smile on his face.

"And I have got to do Delacroix's photos this afternoon, which will take an hour or so."

"Yes, I know. Will you be alright with him by yourself?"

"Of course!" She attacked her *pain au chocolat*.

Jacques finished the last morsel of his bread and jam, gulped down what remained of his coffee and stood. "I need to go," he said. Moving round the table he kissed her. "Call me if you need me."

Beth nodded and he was gone.

Before Jacques wheeled his bike out of the garage, he phoned Didier. "Berger wants to talk... I'm on my way into the office now... OK. We also need to re-instate the surveillance at the chalet. Beth will be here in the village alone for as long as this takes... And get the team together too, Didier... Will be there soon."

***

Alone with the remainder of her breakfast, Beth smiled to herself. *Always the policeman, Jacques. You may not wear the uniform anymore, but you're still a policeman.* She shook her head. "And he's never going to be anyone else, is he?"

The quiet solitude punctuated by the odd snippet of birdsong was her only response. She glanced at her watch; she had a couple of hours before Marie Mancelle arrived.

She emptied the remaining coffee into her cup. Clearing a space on the table, she took the dirty pots and the *cafetière* to the sink. On her way back, she collected her laptop from the snug where she'd left it the night before.

Settled again under the warmth of the canopy that shielded her pale skin from the sun, she waited for the laptop to boot-up.

"So, Monsieur Delacroix, what exactly is it in the top right of your photo." She clicked straight into her software and loaded in the corner containing the odd sign. "Let's see what we really have here."

Like the rest of the photo, the corner she had on screen had already been sharpened. Deciding a further enhancement was necessary she carefully and incrementally made more changes. Zooming in, she examined the remnants of the first line of text, but could make no immediate sense of it. The second line was a series of six letters in full and half of a seventh. The third line was easier as it was in standard sentence case and she could make out the first three words almost in their entirety. The final line was a number: 193.

She frowned. "A postcode? Beginning of a postcode?" She thought for a moment as she munched on the final piece of her *pain*. "If it is the beginning of a postcode, then I might be able to look it up." She did a search on her laptop and stared at the very confusing result.

"I need to be more methodical." She saved the enhanced picture and then enlarged it so that she could see the wording fully. Going back to the first line, she typed out various capital letters for comparison on a blank document she had open in a small separate window at the bottom of her screen. Within moments the possibilities were narrowed down to 'K', 'O', 'R', and 'U'.

The second line appeared to contain more than one word but only the first was visible.

"That's definitely a noun or a verb." When she looked at the wording in the third line and dismissed all other thoughts, a completely different idea came to her.

"Who died? Where and why did they die?"

She shuddered as she realised that the photo may have been taken in a graveyard. Delacroix's comment about his family came back to her. She closed the laptop down.

"I should be ashamed of myself. Prying into another person's private history." She shoved the laptop back in its case and zipped it up so fast she broke a nail.

"Ouch!"

Still sucking her finger, she went to answer the front door to the postman. "Jean-Paul, how are you?"

"Well, thank you. I have something important for you that needs a signature." He handed her a large brown envelope along with a couple of smaller items.

Beth recognised the handwriting. "The final papers for the house," she said as she signed for the post. "Thanks Jean-Paul."

"*À bientôt.*" Jean-Paul ambled down the path to the gate.

saturday, june 18th, 10.00am

Maxim and Amélie were already at their respective desks when Jacques walked into the main office.

"Didier not here yet?"

"He's doing a coffee run. Back in a minute," said Maxim.

Jacques pulled the chair out from behind a spare desk and sat down just as Didier returned with a cardboard tray of four coffees from the place across the road.

"All right," said Jacques as Didier gave out the drinks. "Last night, Chef Berger was still holding out on us. Today, he wants to talk. But he's stipulating conditions. I fully intend to meet him but not alone as he is suggesting."

"You'll need a wire, then," said Maxim.

Jacques nodded. "I'll also want back up. Where are we with the further investigation into Madam Beaufort's background?"

"We're still digging," said Amélie. "But I'm having difficulty bridging the gap between her time at school and 1950 when we know she was in or near Le Puy. She just seems to disappear."

Jacques tried to hide his disappointment by taking a gulp of his coffee. Reminding himself that both Amélie and Maxim were still relatively new to investigative work, he posed a question. "What exactly do we know, and can we use the facts that we already have to make some safe assumptions?"

Amélie frowned and then referred to her notes. "When Henriette was fifteen, she was pulled out of her school in December that year. The school doesn't exist any more, so I've only got basic attendance records that are available in the archives in Paris. I've had those searched and her last day of attendance was Thursday, December 12th. Her name remains in the attendance registers until the following January, when the new term began. In January, she is just not named at all."

"And her younger sister? I believe they both attended the same school," said Jacques.

"Yes, they did, and she's still there in January."

Jacques frowned. "Henriette was fifteen, so that would be 1940. And if her sister was still at school, then I think we can assume that the family, as a whole, had not moved out of the city. Paris was occupied in June 1940, and in chaos at that time. People were trying to leave; had been for months before the occupation."

Amélie nodded. "The next time we have been able to find any record for her is ten years later, and you've already seen that report of the birthday party in Le Puy."

"And what about that inconsistency in the birth registrations for Jean-Charles and Antoine?"

Amélie flicked through her notes. "That might be a dead-end, I'm afraid. Jean-Charles was born in Le Puy in 1963; his birth was registered a week later, also in Le Puy. Antoine's birth in 1965 was recorded in Compiègne because Henriette was in a maternity home there for a month before the birth. The maternity home stopped taking admissions at the end of 1966 and the building was sold in 1967 because the convent attached to it was closed. The remaining nuns were moved to their motherhouse in the centre of Paris. I have contacted the motherhouse, but they weren't very helpful. I couldn't even get a straight answer from them about whether they have the old records or not."

"An estranged wife as well as an estranged daughter," Jacques frowned as he verbalised his thought. "Why would you go all that way to have a baby?"

"If Monsieur Beaufort knew Antoine wasn't his child from the outset, perhaps he didn't want the local press to know. I've checked the newspapers and there was no family announcement of Antoine's birth as there was for his older brother, Jean-Charles," said Amélie.

What else did you and Charles Beaufort agree, Henriette? I wonder what else? Jacques was so lost in his own thoughts he had no idea his colleagues were almost frozen whilst waiting for his response.

He snapped out of his mental machinations. "OK, keep looking. And I agree with you, Compiègne is a long way to go to have a baby. Can we get someone in Paris to search local newspapers for anything about the convent, the maternity home and the order of nuns? And if you can't find anything about Henriette using her married name, then try her own maiden name or her mother's maiden name."

Amélie made a note.

"Any progress on the photo that we acquired yesterday afternoon?"

"It's posted on all our social media sites and on a number of websites where people post about missing relatives or friends," said Maxim. "I did all of that late yesterday and so far we have…" he clicked through to his office email, "… over 40 replies which I will work through this morning."

"Didier, can we get back to Chef Berger and tell him that I will meet him as he requested, but not until this afternoon. I want as much of this missing information in my possession as possible, and I want you and I to be properly prepared. The location he's chosen is a drovers' hut in the forest between Messandrierre and Châteauneuf. I want us to be there first, Didier, so that we can recce and get somewhere safe for you so that everything that is said is on record."

"I'll speak to IT and get everything we need," said Didier.

"We'll reconvene at 14.00, everyone."

***

Beth sat on the bottom step of the spiral staircase, the large envelope on her knees. She smoothed her hand across the address label on the front. The documents inside, she knew, were important and she would open the envelope, but perhaps not just yet. Lost in her own thoughts, she didn't notice Marie Mancelle was standing outside on the porch. It was the gentle tap on the glass panel that caused Beth to look up. She beckoned her neighbour in.

"Beth, are you alright?"

She shook her head. "Not really." She hauled herself to her feet. "The final papers for the house have arrived," she said, staring at the envelope. "So that's it. That's the last link in the chain that binds me to England."

"Isn't that a good thing? Or is it that you aren't happy here?"

"Of course not." Her retort felt a little forced. When Beth looked at Marie directly, she could see in her eyes that she had noticed too. "I'm blissfully happy with Jacques. We just seem to fit. But selling the house… It's so final. And it's not so much the property itself, it's just… Well, it feels like I'm cutting myself off from my home. And no matter how much time I spend here, England will always be my home. It's like when you get married and you leave your parent's home to move into your own house. Your parents' house, the place where you grew up, is always your home, isn't it?"

Marie smiled. "I know what you mean. Moving to another country is a very big change for anyone. But you've managed it well. At least, that's how it seems to me."

"It hasn't always felt like that." Beth moved towards the kitchen. "Come on, I'll make some coffee and we'll sit out on the patio."

"That's better," said Marie. "You're smiling again."

Beth tossed the envelope onto the kitchen worktop and grabbed the *cafetière*.

"And I have some news of my own," said Marie as Beth reached into a cupboard for cups and saucers which she set out on a tray in front of her.

"Is this about the adoption?"

Marie settled herself on a stool. "Yes, everything is going well, and I think Célestine will be with us permanently from the end of summer."

Beth looked up from her task. "Marie, that's wonderful." She filled the *cafetière* with boiled water, added it to the other items on the tray and walked towards the nook. "Come and tell me all about her, and then we'll talk about the music."

***

In the old town in Mende, Delacroix waited for the dealer in the coin and militaria shop to finish his sale to a man and what appeared to be his grandson.

"Monsieur?" The shop owner peered over his counter at Delacroix.

"I was here a few days ago with a list of coins for you to consider," said Delacroix.

"List?" The old man's face crumbled into a questioning look. "List. Yes I remember, now where did I... Ah. Yes." He located the pages and began to leaf through it.

"There's little to be made from coins, you know, Monsieur. They have a melt-down value, of course, which is very small. Most of yours are good only for that. Some I may be able to sell on to youngsters like the lad who has just left. To such as he, the coins are a treasure but in reality the value is often less than when the coin was legal currency."

"So there's nothing of any worth?" Delacroix had to admit to himself that he was disappointed by this response.

"I didn't say that, Monsieur." The old man laid the list on the counter and pushed it across to his customer. "You have 463 coins on that list. There are eleven that may interest me. But I will need to see them and condition will greatly impact any valuation. I have noted which ones they are. There are a further thirty-four that have a value of the agreed minimum level of €10 each or slightly above. Again, I have noted the list. However, there are seventeen commemorative coins that I think may be worth further research."

"And what does that mean, exactly?" Delacroix was

beginning to feel that he had wasted his time, and he couldn't be bothered to keep his irritation from colouring his tone of voice.

"I would need to research the number produced. A small pressing would ensure a reasonable to a good price. As would a registered number and any supporting paperwork. An extensive pressing and the coin is likely to be of little value. The quality of the pressing, any wear and tear would all affect any final value that was attributed." The dealer offered a half smile as he sank back onto the stool he kept just for himself behind the counter.

"OK," said Delacroix as he flicked through his list of coins, now with the dealer's added notes. "I may be back," he said folding the list and secreting it in the inside pocket of his jacket.

In the farmhouse in Messandrierre, an hour or so later, Delacroix was carefully sorting through the box to find the items that were of most interest to the dealer. He had noticed, of course, that the old man had not put any form of valuation against the coins on the list that had particularly interested him. What had been disappointing, though, were the relatively few coins that had any sort of value at all. As he picked out the last that he needed he comforted himself with the thought that his business associate in Rabat couldn't swindle him.

"Neither will you, old man," he said to himself. "Now that I know what I'm dealing with, I can check all this lot out on the web." He grinned to himself as he moved to his desk to begin his searches.

saturday, june 18th, 14.00

Jacques and his team were all together in his room for what he hoped would be the final briefing for the day.

"All the equipment we need is ready and waiting for us, Jacques, including the wire for you," Didier said. "We just need to agree when we will meet Berger."

Jacques glanced at his watch. "Tell him 16.00, and as soon as we've got all the latest information, we'll head out to the agreed location. Amélie and Maxim, what else do we know now?"

"I've done more searches and made some phone calls since this morning," said Amélie. "I can find nothing for Henriette Claudine de Garmeaux or anyone with her christian names reversed. But I have found a listing for a baby Le Bresco in the records of the maternity home in Compiègne. I have also checked their records again for Antoine Beaufort's birth and there is another interesting anomaly. Antoine's birth was recorded on April 2nd at 19.24. But on the next page there is another birth recorded at 19.48. But look at the name." She passed Jacques a copy of the page that had been scanned and emailed to her.

"That's most interesting," said Jacques. "What about the convent and the maternity home, anything of interest there?"

"There is something I've come across," said Maxim. "It was an issue that was reported in the newspapers for quite a few weeks around the time the convent and the maternity home were closed." He handed out copies to everyone. "There were a number of accusations, including physical abuse and forced child labour."

"So why would someone of Henriette's standing and

wealth go to such a place to have her second baby?"

"Perhaps she knew that certain arrangements or accommodations could be made," suggested Didier.

Jacques looked at his colleague. "And she would only know that was possible if she already knew of the place or if she'd been there before. Check further back, Amélie. Check as far back as 1940, assuming they have records from that time."

***

Beth arrived at Delacroix's farmhouse just as the church clock struck the hour.

Delacroix was sitting on the porch waiting for her, dressed in a smart pair of suit trousers with a blue shirt. He led her down to his working space in the old cellar. Beth took in the room. The red of the feature wall was a shade too bright, the painting on the wall had to be a copy and the table, the desk and monitors just looked ostentatious to her.

"The centre of my business world," announced Delacroix. "I was thinking, some pictures of me actually working, sitting behind the desk, and then maybe something less formal in front of the painting or perhaps—"

Beth's eyes widened. "The painting? Are you sure about that?"

"Yeah, why not?" Delacroix moved over to where she stood. "Cost a lot of money, that painting."

More fool you! She gathered her thoughts. "It's a beautiful piece of art, but it is a copy. You did know that when you bought it, didn't you?"

"Hell, yes."

"And the light, the way the light in here reflects on the colours in the oils means that the yellows used to create the flesh tones are heightened. In addition, the dusky pink of the drapes at the back left of the picture are competing with the dark red of the wall and it's creating an imbalance. In the National Portrait Gallery in London, where the original hangs, the background and the frame are more...

140

complementary." She could feel her neck getting warm. "I'm sorry... I shouldn't be so critical."

"I guess this means you know all about art, too."

Beth recovered her composure. "I know a copy of a masterpiece when I see one. Anyone seeing that painting in a photo in the magazine article about you will also know it to be a copy."

"And you think that means I'll be seen as a fraud, is that it?"

Yes, that's exactly what I think, but I can't tell you that. Beth moved in front of the painting and looked around for a better setting.

"I think we should, perhaps, position you at that side of the table," she said pointing to the chair that was furthest away from her. "The pale unobtrusive background will enable the reader to focus on your face. The dark blue shirt you're wearing will contrast well and we can set a few items on the table to make it look like you are working."

Without waiting for his permission, she strode across to Delacroix's desk, picked up a pile of papers, a mobile phone and a small framed photograph of a little girl. She arranged them on the table. It was only as she was positioning the photo that she realised there was something familiar about it. *Must make sure I get a clear shot of that.*

"If you can sit down, please?"

Delacroix nodded and pulled out a chair and sat.

Beth put her bag on the floor, took out her camera and the lens she wanted to use. When she had the camera ready, she began to line up the first few shots. "OK. I just need to re-angle that chair and then we're ready."

With everything in place she began to take pictures. "To start with, I just want you to relax and smile and look at me."

The camera clicked as she moved both left and right to get numerous shots. "Now I want you to talk, Mr Delacroix," she said. "I want to make it look as though there is someone else here who is out of shot, then the pictures will have some dynamism."

Delacroix began talking but she didn't listen, her sole interest was getting the shots. Moving around to the head of the table, she instructed him to maintain his seated position but just change the angle of his head. Then she moved back to her original position and took some more shots.

"I want to zoom in on your face now," she said. After taking half a dozen head and shoulder shots she then zoomed in on the framed photo and took half a dozen shots of that.

And I think I've found the answer to my question.

Finally, she zoomed in on Delacroix and asked him to smile.

"OK. I think I have everything I need," she said.

"Do I get to see them right away?"

A moment of panic hit her as she realised she couldn't just download the shots onto her laptop for him to look through as she would have done normally. *He'll see the close ups he doesn't know about.*

"Not immediately, no. I'll go through them all and pick out the best 20 or so and copy them onto a CD for you and drop it off later. You can look through them and then decide which ones you want to send on to the magazine," she said, a broad smile on her face to cover her inner nervousness.

"OK. Great, and thanks."

As she put her camera away she remembered the old photograph that she had enhanced and repaired. "This is the picture you left for repair," she said handing him the CD and the photograph together. "I'll include an invoice for everything when I drop off the final set of images."

"And the pictures of the area? What about those?"

"I already have plenty of those and will include a selection for you." Her camera bag packed, she shrugged. "Anything else?"

Delacroix collected his papers from the table and moved over to his desk.

"Actually, yeah, there is if you can spare me a few more moments of your time."

Beth was suspicious as she moved to follow him out of

his workspace. Delacroix had been inordinately polite since she arrived; his brash and pushy manner from earlier in the week had disappeared.

"Can you tell me what this is about?" She took the stairs to the ground floor slowly.

Delacroix turned as he reached the top step. "Just follow me," he said. "I need some advice and everything will become clear if we go upstairs."

Beth felt a shiver slide down her back as she halted at the foot of the spiral staircase to the upper floor. In the large vestibule at the entrance to the house, she looked up. Delacroix was nowhere to be seen. On her left was the main living space, which had been remodelled as an extensive kitchen, and dining area.

"Up here," said Delacroix as he leaned over from the top of the stairs to her right. Beth took the steps one by one. As she emerged into the attic space, she saw that the room ran the length of the building. On one side was glass and in the centre a wall. The room was furnished with two sofas, a coffee table and a large reclining chair at one end. A wood-burning stove sat in the centre of the wall.

"This is what I need some help with," he said gesturing towards the rails of clothing that were set at one end of the room.

Beth put her camera bag on the sofa and walked towards the clothing. "I don't understand," she said, mesmerised by the quality and the array of items available. She began to look through the rails.

"I found all of this in some suitcases in the attic. Now that all the work on the house is complete I've finally gotten around to sorting through everything that my uncle left, and these clothes were in the suitcases. I don't know what to do with them."

Beth was entranced. Picking out one hanger and then another, examining the garments and checking the labels and then replacing them.

"I see," she said as she continued her exploration before moving onto the second rail.

"These are beautiful clothes, but I'm still not sure what it is you want my help with."

Delacroix put his hands on his hips. "You've just given me my answer," he said. "So, they have a value, then."

"Oh, very much so," said Beth, finally tearing herself away from the garments and facing him. "A costumier might be interested in them as a complete wardrobe, I should think. But there are now outlets on the Internet that buy and sell vintage clothing, and I would say the majority of this stuff fits that description."

"OK. Thanks. That's useful to know. I guess I've got some work to do."

Beth grabbed her camera bag and moved towards the stairs. "I'll leave you to it, then."

Delacroix followed her down to the front door and held it open for her. "And when you drop off the CD with the photos later, will you join me for a drink?"

"That wouldn't be appropriate, Mr Delacroix," she said, as she pulled at the strap of her camera bag with her left hand, making sure that the ring on her finger was obvious. As he stepped aside, she walked out onto his porch and down the drive without looking back.

Back in her own chalet, a coffee on her table-cum-desk in the loft, Beth was looking at the close ups she had taken of the framed photograph she had seen at Delacroix's. The railings behind the girl were the same as the ones on the photo of himself as a boy that she had repaired. And when she looked at the detail, she found the other half of the sign in the top left corner.

"So, I was right," she said to herself. "This is the other half of the torn photograph." She quickly worked to splice the two halves of the picture together. She was now sure that the sign was a street sign. The last line that she had thought was a postcode was in fact a date, 1939 – 1945. The line above also became clear and referred to deaths in camps. The second line was a name, '*Déportés Martyrs*', and without particularly checking she realised that the first line on the sign could only be '*Rue des*'.

"And a search on the Internet will tell me exactly where that is."

saturday, june 18th, 15.00

Jacques arrived at the appointed meeting place an hour early on foot. He'd left his motorbike in the provided parking at the beginning of the main forest walk.

He quickly checked the area surrounding the old drovers' hut. At the back there was thick scrub that snaked up the exterior wooden wall to the sloping roof. *Not easy for anyone to get up there*. At the front was the narrow path through the forest that intersected with the main forest track to the west about 300 metres away. Smooth worn earth that had been walked by drovers for centuries. He looked left and right into the dense forest, then checked his watch, *Didier should be here soon*. Reaching for the door of the hut, he pulled it open. A cloud of dust – decayed forest debris – swirled out and around his face, almost grateful to be free at last. He coughed and took a couple of steps back. Once the air had cleared, he walked inside. A damp musty smell, like autumn and spring together, hit his nostrils. He let his eyes adjust to the different light. The hut was about four metres by two metres. A small three-legged stool and a low truckle bed were the only furniture. The floor was earth and old straw that had been well trodden together. In a small ring of stones a fire had been created and left to die. Jacques examined the remains. Kids, one weekend, months ago, he thought.

Emerging into the dappled sunlight of the forest he saw Didier on his mountain bike a little way down the path. Jacques waited for him.

"What have we got?" Asked Didier as he dismounted.

"Small, no niceties and no room for unwanted guests," said Jacques

146

"Doesn't mean Berger won't arrive without some, anyway."

"You're right. We need to find a close but hidden spot for you and your bike. I suggest at the back. There's a thicket and a dip behind it." Jacques walked round the hut, Didier following.

"Perfect," said Didier as he began teasing out some of the undergrowth. He stashed his bike at one side of the dip and pushed the undergrowth over and around it to camouflage it.

Removing his backpack, Didier sat cross-legged on the floor and began to unpack his listening equipment. With his small laptop resting on his legs and connected to his phone, he signalled to Jacques that he was ready to run a test. Putting his earpiece in, Jacques pulled up the hood on his jacket and went back into the hut.

"Can you hear me, Didier?"

"Loud and clear."

"OK," said Jacques, "now we wait." He moved out of the hut and stood at the entrance, constantly checking both left and right for anyone who might be on the track. The only sound the susurration of the leaves in the trees as a gentle breeze moved through.

Five minutes before the appointed time Jacques moved into the hut.

"We've got company, approaching from the east," came the whispered warning from Didier a few seconds later. "And it looks like Berger is not alone."

Jacques got up and moved to the open door. "Chef Berger, you wanted to meet."

Berger nodded and moved aside to let the person with him enter the hut first. Jacques remained still and unfazed. He looked at the man in front of him and recognised who it was. The introduction became superfluous.

"This is Antoine Beaufort," Berger said as he followed in behind and seated himself on the edge of the truckle bed.

"At last we meet," said Jacques offering him his hand to shake. "So why all this secrecy?"

147

"It's essential," pleaded Antoine. "You must stop looking for me, Monsieur Forêt. You have to convince my mother to stop looking for me."

"It's not that simple," said Jacques. "If you didn't die in the restaurant fire in Montbel, then someone else did. The police will need to properly identify the body. That case will have to be re-opened."

"You can't allow that to happen, Monsieur." Antoine's tanned and weathered face creased into an earnest frown.

"I have no choice, Monsieur Beaufort. I am an ex-policeman. A man was burned alive in a fire two years ago. He has to be identified. We know the fire was set deliberately. There's the possibility of a murder charge. I cannot, I will not ignore that. There is also the murder of Étienne Vauclain, for which no culprit has been apprehended yet. Do you know anything about that?"

"No." Antoine snapped out his answer.

"I see. The murder weapon, a knife, has been recovered. There was a partial fingerprint on it. Are you sure you don't know anything about Vauclain's murder?"

"Yes! I'm sure. I couldn't stand the man, but that doesn't mean that I would murder him, does it?"

"The police have checked the partial print on the weapon with those they already hold on file. The fire, in which you were supposed to have been killed, didn't obliterate all traces of evidence. The forensics team were able to collect some fingerprint evidence from the body. The partial print on the knife that was used to murder Vauclain matches very closely with the fingerprint evidence taken from the body in the fire at Montbel. Can you explain that?"

Antoine scraped his hands across his face. He glanced at Berger.

"We can't keep hiding any longer, Antoine. Tell him everything."

"All right." Beaufort let out a deep sigh. "You first went to see Vauclain on Thursday the ninth. He called Jonnie straight after you left to alert us of your interest. He also said that he knew you by reputation, and that you wouldn't stop until you found me. As always, he wanted more money. Everything about that man was about money. Jonnie went to the bank and on the Saturday morning I went out to Montbel to see him. Yes, we argued and yes, I did pick up one of the knives and threaten him with it. But I didn't kill him. I swear to God that I didn't kill him."

Jacques looked at Antoine. His face, his demeanour told him that what had just been said was the truth. But that partial match on the fingerprint scratched away at the edge of his mind.

"The fire in Montbel, two years ago. How do you explain your wallet being there? And how do you explain your prints being lifted... Unless you have or did have an identical twin?"

"I did have an identical twin that my mother gave up for adoption. If you have the right amount of money you can buy anything, Monsieur Forêt. He was there in Montbel, not me." Antoine sank down on the floor. "When I left home it was because I'd finally found out what my mother had done. I spent a number of years trying to trace my brother and eventually found him in Indonesia. We spent some time together until I realised he was running drugs but using my name. So I got out fast and didn't tell him where I was going."

"And he found you again through the magazine article, is that it?" Jacques wondered out loud.

"He turned up at the restaurant late, the evening of the fire," said Chef Berger. "I knew who he was as soon as I saw him. Antoine had been helping me in the back creating a final inventory for Vauclain. I let him in."

"And then what?" Jacques addressed his question to Antoine.

"There was no brotherly hugging or greeting. I told him to leave but he wouldn't. We bought him off with some money that was still in the safe from the last day of opening. We left him there overnight to sleep and I went back to Les Alpiers with Jonnie. It wasn't until the next day that I realised I'd left my wallet."

"And all the secrecy?"

"I had to disappear because my brother had been swindling the people he was carrying drugs for."

"And a report of your death in a tragic accident would have enabled you to live a relatively normal life somewhere quiet without having to look over your shoulder all the time. Was that your thinking?" Jacques watched them both closely.

"That was my idea," said Berger. "Once I'd heard about the fire, I persuaded Vauclain to lie for us."

"And that has been costing you ever since, hasn't it?"

Berger nodded. "But I did not kill that man. I may have wanted to, but I did not kill him."

"Neither of us had anything to do with his death," added Antoine.

"That's true," said a voice. A tall man, revolver in hand, stood in the doorway. "He was still alive when we called on Monsieur Vauclain to collect some money he owed us. All three of you move over there." He indicated with the gun that they shift to the back of the hut. "Slowly, put your hands on your heads."

Jacques recognised the man as Marc Meyer, his tail from the previous week. *I hope you're getting all of this, Didier.* The man in the doorway stepped in and moved to his left to let his colleague enter. Slightly shorter but just as powerfully built, a second man entered the hut, also armed. Jacques identified him as Jean Allard, Didier's tail. The second man moved to his right and a third man entered. Barrel-chested, around 1.70 metres tall and in his late forties, the third man swaggered into the space left by his henchmen.

"A little way off your usual turf, Pascal," said Jacques. He saw instantly he was facing the younger of the two Devereux brothers from Marseille. "Your brother Isidore not with you?" Jacques kept his tone respectful but as light as he could muster considering he was unarmed and under the eye of two of Devereux's thugs. He felt sure there would be a third man with a weapon outside.

"Quiet, Forêt," said Devereux. "I'm not interested in you, but get in my way and that could change. It's Beaufort I want. We have a little piece of business to settle, don't we, Beaufort? A matter of some money outstanding."

Antoine tried to step back into the wall of the hut, his face ashen. "No! Please, it wasn't my fault. It's not me you want."

"Bring Beaufort and deal with these two," said Devereux as he took two steps back and a third man, holding a gun, took his place. Jacques didn't recognise him, but he felt sure he would be in police records somewhere.

Allard lunged at Beaufort as his companion, Meyer, pistol-whipped Berger across the face. The chef hit the ground hard and was out cold, blood seeping from the split skin at the side of his face. Jacques remained absolutely still under the stare of the third man. He was waiting for any possible moment that might give him the upper hand. Antoine was pushed to the floor and Allard was holding him down with his knee. He roughly pulled Antoine's arms round his back and secured a tie-wrap tight around his wrists. Meyer and Allard manhandled Beaufort to an upright position and half-marched, half-dragged him out of the hut.

The third man kept his gun trained on Jacques as his two colleagues left with Beaufort.

"Don't follow." He took a step back towards the doorway. "And just to make sure—"

A shot rang out. Jacques hit the ground.

***

Didier froze when he heard gunfire. His first instinct was to get up. But that would blow his cover. He waited. Jacques would give him a sign as soon as he could. Didier kept listening for what seemed an eternity.

"All clear," said Jacques, and Didier raced round to the front of the hut. Jacques was on the floor, lying across the threshold, holding his right upper arm, blood on his jacket, leaking out between his fingers.

"They went that way," he said, indicating along the trail that went west.

Didier put his rucksack on the ground and pulled out a scarf. He wrapped it around Jacques' arm as tightly as he could. Then he moved to Berger who was just beginning to stir, the side of his face red and beginning to swell. Didier took one look at him.

"You'll live," he said.

"Take care of Berger and call this in. Make sure you speak to Pelletier. I need to follow those guys."

Didier retrieved his mountain bike and let Jacques take it. He watched as Jacques, right arm held across his waist, hung on to the centre of the handlebars and pedalled after Devereux and his men. He knew they would have a vehicle waiting somewhere close, probably on the main forest track.

Didier got out his phone and dialled Pelletier.

***

Jacques cycled down the track. The throbbing pain in his arm was getting worse. He was about 200 metres behind Devereux and his men, Antoine being dragged with a gun at his head.

They'll meet the main forest track soon. Jacques eased off on his speed. He needed to keep Antoine and Devereux's mob in sight but remain far enough distant so that they could not hear him. *Don't look round. Just don't look.* The thought became his mantra as he regulated his speed and his breathing. He hit a thick tree root and almost came off the bike. He had to use his right arm to steady himself. The surge of pain ripped through his arm to his shoulder. He forced himself on. *Almost at the main track.*

Antoine stumbled and fell. Jacques veered off the track and into the trees. *One second, two seconds…* Slowly, he peered out. They were moving again. He waited. A few more metres and they were out on the main forest route and heading south.

Jacques got back on the bike and sped towards the

152

turning. *There'll be a vehicle close by. Got to get there. Got to.* His arm was bleeding again and the pain was coming in ever increasing waves of intensity. As he hit the main track he dived into the ditch on his left. He scrambled along. He could hear Antoine's screamed protestations. He willed him to keep fighting. He just needed to edge a little closer.

A car door slammed. Then another. *A bit closer.* A third door slammed. *Last chance.* Jacques raised himself so that he could see above the edge of the ditch. The vehicle pulled away. Jacques fell back into the ditch, the water seeping into his clothes, his breathing heavy. He closed his eyes, just for a second, he told himself.

saturday, june 18, 18.00

Beth had finished the work for Delacroix. Her last task was to type a list of all the photographs that she had put on the CD. She saved the list onto the disc, extracted it from the drive on her laptop and then returned it to the case, which she had already labelled.

Having changed her mind about putting the CD through Delacroix's post box, she grabbed her camera bag, keys and jacket and set off to walk across to his place.

She had already thought out what her story would be and had rehearsed it in front of the bathroom mirror a few times. She wouldn't be as good as Jacques at this sort of thing, she knew that, but at least she could try. *I've got to try.* She passed the dead oak and turned down the short path that lead to *Ferme* Delacroix.

She didn't need to knock. Delacroix sat on his porch in the warm evening sunshine. Her mind shifted to English as she presented him with what she hoped was her best smile.

"I see you've your camera. Does this mean the first lot of photos are no good?"

"No, Mr Delacroix, the first—"

"Call me Ricky, unless you're going to bill me for this too?"

"No, I'm not," she said as she handed him the CD. "But I am here to apologise and to ask if I could take more photos."

Delacroix relaxed back in his chair a broad smile on his face. "I'm listening," he said.

"Everything you need is on the disc including some shots of the surrounding area. However, when I was up in your attic space, I was so distracted by all those beautiful clothes

154

of your aunt's that I didn't realise until I got back home that probably one of the best places to get some shots of the village and the area are looking out from your loft window. I was wondering if you would mind if I did that either now or tomorrow or whenever was most convenient to you."

"You're welcome right now," he said getting up and moving to the open door. "Just go right on up and take your shots, and I'll go and get us something to drink. Is a Sauvignon to your taste?"

Beth nodded and began to mount the stairs. She got her camera ready. Whilst she waited for her host to return she looked at the view from his loft area. The sun was in the right aspect and lighting up the peaks opposite. The various shades of green from the forest and the enclosed fields, jewelled with the bright yellow of the clumps of *genêt*, would create a perfect picture. She was so engrossed in the scenery, she didn't know Delacroix had returned until he was right behind her.

"Great vi—"

Beth started. "Sorry, I was miles away."

"You sure you're OK?" He handed her a glass of wine.

She nodded and took a sip. Putting the glass down on the coffee table, she moved to the centre of the long window. "This view here is stunning and I was thinking that we could have you, in your reclining chair, just here."

"Done," he said. Moving round the room he shifted the furniture to accommodate the change and sat down.

Beth moved away to better line up her shot. "OK. If you could swivel round just a little this way and then look out of the window and hold that..." Her camera clicked away. She moved a little to her left. "OK just hold that pose... That's great OK now look towards the corner of the room and talk... You must have loved being here as a child, tell me about that..." Beth moved and continued to take shots.

"Not really," he said. "I was born in Québec and grew up there. I'd been here, to France, on business a few times but here in the village, my first visit was for old uncle Guy's funeral and—"

155

"OK. I think I really have got everything I need this time, Mr Delacroix." She removed the lens and repacked her camera.

"I'll straighten the room and then we can chat." As he stood Beth glanced at her watch.

"I need to go. Jacques will be home soon. But thanks for your co-operation." She turned and ran down the stairs.

"Any time," he shouted.

Out in the fresh air, she hurried along to the top road. "That photograph is a lie," she said. "And so are you, Mr Delacroix."

**

In the hospital in Mende, Jacques' arm had been x-rayed. There was no damage to the bone, and the doctor had confirmed that the injury was a flesh wound only. Chef Berger's injury was more concerning. He had been admitted so that the damage to his cheek and jaw could be fully assessed and monitored.

At just before 20.00, Jacques was released with instructions, which he had no intention of heeding, and medication, which he would only take when he was sure that Antoine was safe. Outside, Didier was waiting.

Jacques eased himself into the passenger seat, his right arm in a sling. Didier's face blanched white when he saw him.

"Yes, you're right. I feel like shit and probably look like it too." As he reached across for his seat belt he winced with pain.

"And you smell of ditch." Didier shifted into gear and moved off.

"Just update me." Jacques closed his eyes for a moment as another wave of pain hit him.

"The Mercedes in the forest was stolen two days ago in Marseille and the plates came from a Renault that was stolen and then torched two months ago, also Marseille. Pelletier has got his team to make sure all sightings of the vehicle on the CCTV cameras were passed to his incident room and we now know that Devereux, Allard, Meyer and the third man are in a derelict farmhouse on the other side of Mende."

"And Antoine?"

"He's with them, and we are going to meet Pelletier there now." Didier turned onto a D road, which started to climb. Traffic was non-existent and he raced along a fast as he dared. On a sharp bend, he pulled onto a dirt track and slowed down. About 500 metres away lay an entrance to a field. Didier turned into it.

Pelletier was in a large vehicle watching monitors. Like Didier, the magistrate could not hide his reaction to Jacques' appearance.

"You shouldn't be here," he said, turning towards the monitors again.

"You're right, I'm not a policeman any more." Jacques scrutinised the feed that was coming through from the swat team that Pelletier had deployed.

"Antoine has been badly beaten but is still alive. Allard is guarding him at the moment and Devereux, Meyer and the third man – we still haven't a definite ID on him yet – are in another room at the back. We're just waiting for the signal to go."

Moments later, Allard was down, Antoine was surrounded by three of the team, and two more shots were fired. Jacques watched the feed. As Antoine was released from his bindings he slumped forward. One of team put him in the recovery position and checked his vital signs. The waiting rescue vehicle moved on command, lights flashing.

The message came through that all four of the suspects were accounted for. Allard had a wound in the shoulder, Meyer likewise, and the third man was dead. Devereux had bolted but had been stopped by the second level of security outside the property.

Jacques let out a heartfelt sigh of relief. "He's safe. Let's hope his injuries are superficial."

monday, june 20th

Jacques had one last look at the file of papers that he would be handing over to Magistrate Pelletier. His right arm was still painful but his greatest difficulty was having to use his left hand for everything. When Maxim tapped on his door to show Pelletier in, Jacques detailed him to make the coffee.

"I'm not sure that we're going to need your papers, Jacques, but I will take them anyway." The Magistrate tipped three sachets of sugar into his cup, much to Jacques surprise who thought he was still on the diet that had been imposed by his wife.

"The forensics put Meyer in Vauclain's property on the day of the murder."

"I didn't read the whole report when you brought it over, Bruno. So what else was there?"

"A boot print in the garage that is a perfect match for a pair of Meyer's trainers that we recovered from his bin yesterday, and there are traces of blood on them. In addition, we've got their mobile phones and early analysis puts both Meyer and Allard in the vicinity of Vauclain's property both before and after the murder. We need to make further checks but so far the results look promising." Bruno finally stopped stirring his coffee, put his spoon in the saucer and took a drink.

"There is one other thing that you will find interesting," said Bruno. "You suggested to me that there might have been collusion between Vauclain and Luc Nowak over the torching of the restaurant in Montbel two years ago."

"Yes, I did. But, if I remember correctly, you said there was no evidence."

"That's right, Jacques. I could find none. And it is

something that has always made me wonder. Now, I can tell you that it was Meyer who hired Nowak, probably under instruction from Devereux. But we'll never get an admission of that. Vauclain owed a lot of money, and it seems he had upset a lot of the wrong kind of people. The Devereux brothers were only one criminal family on his tail." Bruno picked up his coffee cup and then thought better of it. "There's too much sugar in this." He pushed his cup and saucer away.

Jacques grinned but was too polite to comment. "And if the murder charge for Meyer doesn't stick then at least you have kidnap and grievous bodily harm and probably a few others too."

"Yes, we do. But we also have Devereux's conniving lawyers to deal with."

"He was there at the scene, Bruno. He must have known what was happening, and must have authorised, or at least been aware of, the action that his thugs would or might take. And don't forget there is the recording from the Drover's hut. It was Devereux himself who issued the order to 'deal' with us in the hut." Jacques' arm was throbbing again. *Maybe the doctors were right. Perhaps I should take some time off.*

"Yes, I know. We will use that as best we can, but I fear that it won't be enough." Bruno stood. "I think you should be at home, Jacques. So, if you have the papers?"

"Of course," said Jacques, handing Pelletier the file. "On a completely different subject, Bruno, I just wanted to let you know that Beth and I are finally getting married at the end of summer. Date still to be finalised, but it would make us very happy if you and your wife would be there."

"Congratulations to you both, and yes, we would be honoured." Bruno stood, papers under his arm and glanced at his watch. "I need to go. We'll look forward to your invitation."

Alone at last, Jacques sank back in his chair and rested his eyes. He still had to see Henriette Beaufort, but he decided that could wait a couple of days or so. But the

Delacroix question that Beth had raised, that couldn't wait. He needed someone working on that right away. He went through to the general office. Didier was out but Maxim and Amélie were there. He sat at Didier's desk.

"I'd like you to do some research, please. Richard Laurent Delacroix, he lives in Messandrierre and claims to be a Canadian national. He also claims to have been born and brought up in Québec. Here is a photograph of him as he looks now. And here is a photograph that he says is him when he was a boy." Jacques passed across one of the headshots Beth had taken at the weekend and a copy of the repaired photo that she'd worked on.

Maxim looked at both photos closely. "What is it that you think we are looking for?"

"I'm not entirely sure. At best, just a misunderstanding. At worst, identity theft, misappropriation, fraud, theft of assets. I really don't know yet. But one thing that Beth is very certain of is that the street on which the boy's photo was taken is in a small town just south east of Rouen. If you look carefully at the background there is a street sign. Beth has checked on the Internet and the street is actually there."

Amélie frowned. "Perhaps he visited when he was child. Does he have relatives here in France?"

Jacques thought back to Delacroix's comments about his family on the day of the formal opening of Beth's shop. "According to him, he is the last of the family. His uncle, Guy Delacroix, died and Richard is the sole surviving relative. If you accept that as being true, why would he lie about his childhood. Either he has something to hide or that photo of the boy is not Richard Laurent Delacroix. If the boy is not Richard, then who is he? And why does Richard have no photos of his own? Whichever way you look at it, there is something not quite right here." Jacques shifted in his chair, the pain in his arm causing him grief.

Maxim nodded. "Where would you like us to start?"

"When Didier comes back, perhaps he could try and get some information from Immigration through his old colleagues. And you both could start with our usual sources:

voting lists, Internet, newspapers, archives, etc. Get me anything you can find on Richard Laurent Delacroix."

His instructions given, Jacques decided that was enough for the day. He collected his bag and took a slow and laboured walk across town to Beth's shop in the hope that she might close up early and drive him home.

wednesday, june 22nd

At the *château*, Madame's assistant was waiting for Jacques to arrive.

"Thank you for coming, Monsieur. Madame is not well today," he said as he began to lead Jacques through the familiar halls to Henriette Beaufort's room. As Jacques entered, he caught the faint smell of illness. Madame's assistant pointed to a door on the opposite side of the room that Jacques had not particularly noticed before.

"She's through there," he said.

Jacques nodded, crossed the sitting room and quietly walked into a bedroom. It was decorated in the same faded and well-worn colours and furnishings as the outer room. Henriette was propped up on the bed with pillows, her head lying back and her eyes closed. She looked to have aged ten years since he had last seen her.

"I'm only resting my eyes, Monsieur Forêt. Please find a chair and sit." Her voice was thin and reedy, but her inner strength still had not left her.

Jacques brought a small armchair from the far side of the room, set it at the side of the bed and sat down.

"My son, have you found my son?"

"I've found all three of them, Madame."

Her eyes flickered open for a moment. "Tell me, tell me everything."

"Your first son, Antoine Le Bresco, was born on June 13th in 1941. The day before your 16th birthday in a maternity home in Compiègne. Like a lot of orphans at that time, he was brought up in the care of the nuns who ran the home. He remained there until he died at the age of fifteen months old." There was a hardness to Jacques' tone that he

162

hadn't intended.

"You're judging me, Monsieur. I can hear it in your voice. You've no right to judge. You've no idea of what it was like back then. Do you know what it's like to be over-run? To be occupied?" She glared at him.

Jacques shook his head.

"Of course you don't, you're far too young. When they came, we felt them first. Through the floors and the walls of the buildings. Then there was the steady low hum, like thunder in the distance. It became louder and louder, and then they were there. Tanks, army vehicles, soldiers everywhere. In that moment, our lives changed forever. The city had been in panic for days, months; we knew they were coming. People had left in droves, but Grandfather refused to leave and kept all of us there."

"And Maximilian?" Jacques looked at the small photo, turned it over and glanced at the dedication on the back.

Für meine einzige wahre Liebe, Max

"Is that true? Were you his one true love?"

Henriette nodded and a tear rolled down her cheek. "It's true; he was the only man I ever loved. But those times were difficult...and desperate. It was Grandfather who separated us, and it was Grandfather who cut me out of the de Garmeaux family. The last thing that evil, selfish old man ever did for me was to buy me my place at the maternity home in Compiègne."

"How did you and Maximilian find each other again?"

Madame reached for her oxygen. "It was chance. Pure chance. I was taking a much-needed break in Monaco in August 1964. Maximilian was living there with his wife and two young children." Henriette paused for a moment and looked away.

"And you couldn't stay with him," surmised Jacques.

"I wanted to. I would have done, but Max felt duty bound to support his family."

"And your husband, Charles?"

"Charles? He hadn't been near me for months and had found himself someone else. But divorce? In the Beaufort family? Charles wouldn't hear of it. We had too much to hide. Just like him, I took what little love I could find, when and where I could. I had two blissful weeks with Max. The following April my second surviving son, Antoine, was born." A tear slid down her cheek.

"But he wasn't your only child, was he? He had a twin brother whom you left at the maternity home for adoption. That second child was registered by the home as Francis Le Bresco. Was that also an 'arrangement' you came to with Charles Beaufort?" Jacques found his anger and resentment was beginning to get the better of him.

"Yes. Charles could be very cruel at times. And when you have money, you can buy anything."

Jacques wanted to spit out his anger, but he looked away and took a deep breath. He reminded himself that there was no point in railing against injustices that he could not change. He could only resolve to ensure that such injustice never occurred again if it was in his power to stop it.

"Your son, Antoine Beaufort, is not too far away," he said when he felt able to continue. "He lives in Les Alpiers. He knows you want to see him and he knows where you are, but I am not certain that he wants to see you."

"Persuade him, Monsieur. Convince him to come, please. I need to tell him I'm sorry."

Jacques had heard enough. He stood, intending to leave, but hesitated for a moment.

"I will forward a bill within the week, Madame." He turned and quietly made his way to the door and left.

Outside in the fresh air again, he took a long look at the driveway stretched out in front of him. Another world, he thought. He glanced back at the *château* and realised he was glad to be away from the place.

"Let's get out of here, Didier," he said as he got back in the car. He had one more task to complete.

He'd instructed Didier to take the mountain roads so that he could be alone with his thoughts. He'd also suggested that his partner might want to make use of the car's power. Jacques had the mental weight of an unpleasant investigation from which he needed to escape. As they raced over passes and through cols with only a fleeting regard for speed, Jacques could feel the darkness gradually beginning to recede. Had he been able to, he would have done this on his bike. He needed the speed. The exhilaration. But Beth had insisted that he take things easy and had called Didier to ensure that Jacques would also follow her wishes.

As they neared Les Alpiers, Didier slowed and, riding into the village, he made sure his speed was legal. He pulled up outside the farmhouse and parked the car inside the wide entrance. The window of the small study next to the front door was open. Jacques smiled to himself as he approached the front door and knocked.

"Monsieur Forêt, I wasn't expecting to see you again," said Antoine Beaufort. The bruising to his face still looked angry and his movement showed that he was also suffering some pain.

"Come in," he said, holding the door wide open. "Go through, I'm in the kitchen. I'm developing some new recipes for Jonnie. It's about all I'm fit for until my ribs mend."

Jacques strode through the house. "Whatever it is, it smells very good."

Antoine moved slowly across the kitchen to his stove, checked a pan and adjusted the heat. "What can I do for you?"

Jacques looked around. *Where to start.* He sighed. "I know you have no wish to see your mother...and I don't judge your decision. It is yours, and yours alone to make."

"We agree on something, then."

Jacques shifted his weight from one foot to the other. "I'm only the messenger, I know that, but I just wanted to make one last observation. Less than two years ago, I got a call from home. But I didn't take it. I was at work and involved in an investigation. I didn't access the voicemail telling me that my mother was close to death until the following day. By the time I got to Paris, it was too late." He pinched the bridge of his nose. "There isn't a day goes by that I do not regret that decision."

He moved to leave and took a step towards the front the door but stopped. He faced Antoine Beaufort again. "I don't want to think that you might make the same mistake, Monsieur."

Antoine remained motionless.

Jacques nodded, and the next second he was gone, striding down the path to where Didier was waiting. He eased himself into the passenger seat.

"I've said what needed to be said, Didier. I can't do anymore. Let's get back to the office. I want to know what the team have found out about Delacroix."

Didier started the car and shifted into first gear. Jacques glanced in the wing mirror. In the window of Jonnie Berger's study, Antoine Beaufort was watching them, mobile phone in his hand.

Monsieur, I sincerely hope you're making the right call, thought Jacques.

THE END

glossary of terms in order of appearance

la lettre	the letter
salle des Fêtes	community room
gîtes	holiday cottage
patisserie	pastry and cake shop
fermier	farmer
maman	mother
cafetière	coffee pot
cave	wine cellar
Chef de Partie	Chef in charge of a particular kitchen station, e.g pastry, fish, vegetables
château	castle, fort or country house
plongeur	kitchen staff employed to wash up
marmiton	kitchen staff employed to wash and maintain pans and equipment
saucier	Chef responsible for sauces – one of the most respected of posts in kitchen
Chef de Cuisine	Head Chef
Police Nationale	National police
papa	dad
gendarmerie	rural police
Mon coeur s'ouvre a ta voix	My heart opens to your voice
Manon	A French opera by Massenet
Au fond du temple saint	At the foot of the holy temple
gendarme	policeman
maire	mayor
boulangerie	baker's shop
boucher	butcher
née	born
petite	small
moiré	watered silk
Breton	language spoken in Brittany

Recettes de Ma Petite Cuisine Cévenole	Recipes from my Little Cévennes Kitchen
hiver	winter
décor	decoration and furnishings
Tarte au Beaufort	Beaufort tart
tartelettes	small round tarts
centimes	100 centimes/cents = €1
département	one of the 90+ specifically named administrative areas of France
tabac	tobacconist, often also a coffee shop and newsagents combined
café	coffee shop
Père Chastain	Father Chastain
Préfecture	administrative centre of a *département*
Épicerie Giroux et Fils	Giroux and Sons, Grocers
Bretagne	Brittany
arrondissement	an area of Paris, equivalent of Chelsea or Islington in London
petites announces	personal ads/announcements
canapés	bite-size nibbles
maître d'	abbreviation for *maître d'hôtel* = steward/butler/head waiter
hirondelle	Swallow
salon	lounge
pique	Spade as in cards
amandine	a pastry case filled with: a layer of marzipan, a layer of almond flavoured sponge, often glazed and decorated with almonds and/or a dusting of icing sugar
rosette	a dry sausage eaten by itself or with small gherkins
fiancé	engaged man
bonjour	hello/good morning
croissants	folded triangles of pastry
baguette	standard loaf

pain au chocolat	rolled pastry layered with chocolate
à demain	until tomorrow
à bientôt	see you soon
rue des Déportés Martyrs	Deported Martyrs' Road
ferme	farm
genêt	a coarse bush-like plant that grows about 2-3 metres in height and is covered in bright yellow flowers in summer.

Fantastic Books
Great Authors

darkstroke is
an imprint of
Crooked Cat Books

- Gripping Thrillers
- Cosy Mysteries
- Romantic Chick-Lit
- Fascinating Historicals
- Exciting Fantasy
- Young Adult and Children's
  Adventures
- Non-Fiction

Discover us online
www.darkstroke.com

Find us on instagram:
www.instagram.com/darkstrokebooks